I'll Always Be Down for My Man

Fallon Kirkland

I'll Always Be Down for My Man

Copyright © 2017 by Fallon Kirkland

Published By: Grand Penz Publications

Text GrandPenz to 22828 to stay up to date with new releases, sneak peeks, contest, and more...

Text **SPROMANCE** to 22828 to stay up to date on new releases, plus get information on contests, sneak peeks, and more!

.

.

Acknowledgments

I want to thank God, first and foremost, for the beautiful-blessing he has given me. Without him, none of this is possible. I always and forever will thank my Guardian-Angel, (My Mother) Dorothy Ann Kirkland, better known as (Dot).

If only God had visitations in heaven, I'd be there every day! I love you mom, more than word could ever express. Tears are now falling as I write… Mom, thank you for watching over me. I feel your presence every day. I love you Angel! My dedications won't be right if I didn't mention my kids. My kids are the reason why I write. Their faces bring-out a fight in me from deep-within, and I have no-choice, but to go hard. I love my kids with every piece of my heart.

With I'd also like to give a very loving thanks to my fiancée, Michael Russell. Baby, there's not a word to truly-describe what you mean to me. I love you just the way you are! Thanks for the constant motivation and support you always give. I love you to no end!

I'm just over-blessed to say I'm living in my-gift, (my dream) and it feels absolutely-amazing!! I'm very proud of myself, and I thank the better-me for not giving up. I'm proud of the woman I've become, and I must thank God, because of that! If it wasn't for him shinning his bright-flashlight at a dark-time in my life and leading me out the darkness, I'd still be stuck with a dream and doubts. Year

2016, was an interesting year for me, from releasing my first book and the death of my mother, but I'm blessed to say I've made it-though… Now, here's to more strength, less-stress and more blessings for the New-Year and through-out. I also want to thank my publisher Monique for all she's done in assisting me… (*Thank you!*) You are truly-appreciated! -And thank you to everyone that supported me in anyway, you know who you are! Thanks again! And as always, be on the lookout for more great books to come.

Love,

Author Fallon L Kirkland (DOT'S

Daughter)

Table of Contents

PROLOGUE

"What the fuck is going on?" I shouted as I witnessed my husband on his knees with his face buried deep into this stank bitch's pussy.

"Baby, it's not what you think?" my husband stuttered as I watched him wipe her slimy pussy juices from his mouth.

My body had immediately frozen. Deep inside my mind, I already knew Rashad was still cheating, but I didn't want to believe it. Now the truth was staring me dead in the face, along with the smell of dead fish. The smell of dead-fish, woke me from the trance I was in, as the funky smell burnt my nostrils.

I knew, at that very moment, I was going to kill my husband and his dirty ass side-bitch...

"Baby, just calm down!" Rashad trembled while his eyes bulged from his eye socket when I pulled my Beretta from my Louis Vuitton handbag. I pointed it directly at my husband's head as he became very stiff while he nervously awaited my next move. As I looked over to observe his ghetto side-chick, she was somehow smiling as she pulled her blonde micro braids from her face...

"Umm, excuse me?" This bitch had the nerves to say as she raised her hand like she was a two-year old child.

"Bitch! What the *fuck* do you want?" I said through my teeth as my anger enhanced from the sight and smell of her dirty ass!

"Well… since everything is already laying on the table, I just think you should also know that I'm pregnant too!" she revealed as she proudly exposed her open-face gold grill…

That was all I remembered before my bedroom became a crime scene, blocked-off with yellow-tape…

THE BEGINNING

"Tia, cross your legs and sit like a lady!" My mother would always remind me along with the other million-and-one rules of being a lady...

You see, I was raised to be a lady, but most importantly... I was raised to become someone's wife one day. I was taught a wife should always have their husband's back, through thick or thin. I was taught this lesson by example, because my mother was the type of wife any man would dream of! She made sure my daddy had full-course meals on the table every night. She also made sure the house was spic and span, and me and my brother were in bed by 8:30 sharp! I remember how she would wait up for daddy in her silk night gown, sweet smelling perfume and a face full of makeup, although, she didn't need it. My mother was a beautiful woman! She was what the old folks would call a brickhouse. She had the coldest coke bottle figure with eyes of a fox. She also had the sharpest cheek bones with thick sensual lips. She reminded folks of Lena Horne. Her hair was naturally long, and very fine. It almost reached her amazing back side. Unfortunately, as beautiful as mom was, daddy never made it home at night. He would always come strolling in the next morning with lipstick on his collar, right before it was time for us to go to school. I remember the pissed off expression mom would have on her face when she saw him coming through the door.

3

"Sweet thang, I'm home!" Dad would always say with a trifling grin on his face.

Mom would somehow force a smile on her face, even though her smudged makeup recorded the truth. She had been crying all night. For some strange reason, mom always swallowed her pride, and would always ask if he was hungry. Not once, would she ask where the *hell* he'd been. Like I said before, my mother was a wife that really loved her husband. She loved her husband so damn much, she even took in three of daddy's outside kids. His scandalous ass mistress abandoned those bastards on our front porch one cold night without a pair of shoes on their feet. Any woman would have chunked the deuces up and divorced daddy right then, but not my mother. She stuck with my daddy through hell and high water. When daddy had lost his job after he caught a sudden case of pneumonia, my mother worked doubles to make ends meet. Twenty-five years would have marked their anniversary today, except my mother and father would never have the chance to see it. Sadly, my mother and daddy contracted AIDS from daddy's infidelities. Even when my mother found out she was sick, she still didn't divorce my father. I guess she strongly believed in "Till death do us part."

CHAPTER 1

Today, I sit in prison waiting on my husband to show. I often think about how powerful love really is, and how loving someone can make you do crazy things. I've been locked down for five-years now, and it's all because of love. Although, I'm not complaining, I just wish things could have been handled differently. You see, I'm doing ten-years for a manslaughter I didn't commit. But, like I said before, love will put you into situations you never imagined. I sit behind these prison walls now at twenty-nine years old. I often think, how could I love a man more than I love myself? I also ask myself was it even worth it. I had so much ahead of me. I had just passed the state boards as a registered nurse. I had just gotten married, and I was expecting my first child with the love of my life, my husband Rashad. I was so in love, and happier than I could ever be. I was living the real-life story of Beauty and the Beast, because I was that good girl that had fallen for the beast… Except, Rashad was as fine as they come, and he was truly a beast when it came to the streets.

In the beginning, I tried to resist Rashad, especially with his bad-boy reputation. But, it was something about Rashad that struck my curiosity. I don't know if it had anything to do with his good looks, his diamond-chains, the cars he drove, or the fact that he was heavily respected? Either way, I just had to have him, and I did just that. Being with Rashad wasn't easy though, because I had many dealings with his side-chicks. They just couldn't accept the fact that Rashad was now with me, even with the big-ass tattoo of my name across his back. Those starving hoes just wouldn't let us be! I guess it was hard to say so-long to their perfect man, because Rashad really was the perfect man. His respect was never challenged, money wasn't shit to him, and his dick game was superb! Just as I was reminiscing on the special times in my life, Tonya, (the prison-guard) called my name for visitation.

"Tia King!" she shouted as I gracefully walked the long hallway that would soon lead me to Rashad. As I walked, I watched as Tonya cut her beady-eyes, the minute she saw me coming. She had a permanent look on her face as if she had smelled shit.

Tonya was once one of Rashad's side-chicks he had dogged in the past. I guess she decided to change her lifestyle by moving to these boondocks. They never lied when they say it's a small world! Honestly, I didn't care, because Tonya was before my time and long if she knew who Rashad belonged too, we were cool. Besides, I was just happy to be seeing my husband after a long six months, and I refused to let anything kill my happiness.

I wanted to jump up and down as we got closer to the conjugal room. I missed Rashad so much, and I couldn't wait to feel his flesh against mines. I was extremely horny, and I couldn't wait to feel Rashad's massive-dick. I could feel my vagina pulsating in excitement. My vagina was dripping wet when we finally made it to the conjugal room that was reserved for me and my husband. As I walked over to Rashad, Tonya's eyes rolled as she informed us that we had only one hour and slammed the door behind her. Little did she know, one-hour was more than enough time. I didn't waste any time pulling-down my prison uniform and spreading my legs wide while Rashad whipped-out his hard erection and pushed-it deep inside my tight, and extra-wet vagina.

"Umm!" Rashad and I both moaned, as our bodies connected as one. Tears ran from my eyes while Rashad continued to penetrate me. His dick was so huge, but it also felt so damn good that it took my breath away.

"Oh God... Yes, baby!" I panted while gasping for air as Rashad enhanced the speed of his powerful-strokes.

"Hell yeah! Fuck me baby!" I cried out, as I felt my vagina go numb. I soon unleashed my orgasm while Rashad immediately joined me. Rashad and I had come to a mind-blowing orgasm as his heavy-cream sank deep into my starving pussy. I immediately closed my eyes like a strung-out junkie that had just been blessed with the best dope out, Rashad's dick. I gratefully smiled, as I thanked him for quenching the drought I had between my thighs. Those two-minutes was perfect! Usually we would be longer, but we really missed each other, and we had a lot of catching up to do.

"So, how's Junior?" I immediately asked, as I pulled-up my prison uniform.

"He's good," Rashad replied as he quickly zipped his pants.

"So, how have you been?" I asked, as I suspiciously cut my eye at him.

"Everything's cool," he responded, while he stared at the prison's floor. I knew whenever Rashad looked down at the floor, it was usually a sign that something was clearly wrong.

"Well, everything doesn't seem cool, being that you haven't visited me in almost five-months?" I didn't waste any time confronting him while I folded my arms awaiting his explanation.

"Tia, don't start that shit!" he warned, as he got up and began to pace the floor.

"Looks like you got a lot on your mind. What's up?" I asked, as I watched how he continue to pace the floor very nervously.

"Listen Tia, I didn't want to tell you like this, but I guess there's no other way to tell you."

"Tell me what?" I asked, as I now felt my heart began to beat very heavily. I watched as Rashad took a deep breath before he spoke again.

"Tia, you know I'll always love you, but I feel that our time has expired, and I don't want to do this anymore," he surprisingly spoke. At that moment, I felt my heart shatter into thousands of little pieces.

"What are you saying, Rashad?" I squealed as my throat began to burn, as I tried to swallow down the hurt I was now feeling.

"I'm saying I want a divorce," he shockingly revealed, as he finally looked at me for the first time.

"A divorce? What the fuck you mean a divorce?" My voice cracked as I began to panic. I stared at Rashad who now looked blurry from all the tears that had formed in the webs of my eyes.

"Come on Tia, you've been gone for five-years. What did you think would come of this?"

"Fuck you, Rashad! I'm here because of you... remember?" I reminded him as my heart pumped with anger and pain from Rashad's startling confession.

"See, that's what I'm talking about. Here you go, bringing up that past shit again!" he cringed, while he looked over at me as if I was overreacting.

"What the fuck you mean, the past?" I fumed, as I slowly walked over to him, just in case Tonya had been listening. "I'm doing ten-years because of you! And all you can tell me is, it's the past? Are you fuckin crazy?" I had asked him, because there was no way in hell this nigga could be sane. I watched as he slowly nodded his head to confirm that he was indeed insane.

"I can't believe you, Rashad!" I shouted as I shook my head in astonishment. "Something that's the past for your ungrateful-ass, is an everyday reality for me!" I immediately

9

reminded him as I pointed at the bright-orange prison uniform I'd been wearing for five-years now.

"I understand, and I'm very grateful for you doing that. But, I can't continue to put my life on pause, because you're in here," Rashad tried to explained. Before he could finish what, he was saying, I had slapped him across his face extremely hard as my anger intensified at a record high.

"Excuse me, what about my life?" I scorned as Rashad rubbed the side of his stinging cheek.

"Tia, I didn't come here to argue with you. I come to tell you it's over!" Rashad shouted-out the hurtful news without any regards to my feelings.

"I'll still keep plenty money in your commissary, but me and you are over!" he assured, as he looked me directly in the face without even an ounce of shame.

"Who is she?" That was my only response, as tears fell down the sides of my cheeks.

"She's not you!" Rashad finally spoke as he quickly storms out of the room, leaving me with a wet ass and confused.

A few seconds later, Tonya, (the prison guard), walked-in with some papers at hand.

"Tia, you've officially been served," she proudly spoke, as she handed-over my divorce papers.

I felt my whole world crumble. Everything I was living for was destroyed in that very moment. As I walked back to my cell, I felt very dizzy. I felt like I would pass-out at any second, as I carefully watched my steps as I walked to my lonely cell.

When I finally made it to my cell, I ran to my bunk and buried my face in my paper-thin mattress. I cried so hard, I had passed out! After I finally woke up, I tried my best to gather my thoughts. I had decided to make a call to my best friend, Stacey. I knew if anyone knew what was going on, she would. As I quickly dialed Stacey's number, I was immediately forward to her voice mail…

"Hi! This is Stacey. I'm sorry I can't answer my phone at the time. Go ahead and leave me a message and I'll be sure to return your call… Thank you and God bless, Mwah!"

>Beep<

"Hey Stacey, it's Tia. I haven't heard from you in a while. If you can, please come visit me or write me ASAP… I miss you, bye."

After I left Stacey a message, I hung up the phone and returned to my bunk where I wrote a letter to Rashad.

Rashad,

I haven't talked to you in months. Can you please answer the phone or at least respond to my letters? I'm really missing you! I been wrecking my mind trying to figure out what I had done to deserve this? The only thing I ever done to you, was love you. I'm to the point I can't eat or sleep. Baby, just tell me why are you doing this to me? At least tell me why you want a divorce? I need to know something, because I'm losing my mind in here. I don't think I'll get through these next five-year without you! Please respond to this letter, or better yet, please come see me. I'm dying in here!

Fallon Kirkland

Love you to death! (Your one & only wife),
Tia!

As I wrote, I couldn't help but to wet the letters with my
tears. For the first time, I felt very low and defeated. I did
half of my sentence with a clear mind, but to do another five-
years for an ungrateful-bastard would be hard. After I
finished writing my letter, I enclosed it with my usually kiss. I
laid back on my bunk heartbroken, with so many questions.
But my main question was, *why?*

CHAPTER 2

It'd been three-months since Rashad's last visit. Every visitation, I would always pray he'd show up. But somehow, he'd always leave me disappointed and extremely horny. I suspect he's probably pissed, because I didn't sign those damn divorce papers yet. I guess I still had faith that love would see us through. I'd always dreamt of the day when I could come home and raise my son with my husband, and I still did. I understood how hard it must be for Rashad, especially raising our son all by himself. I understood that he had needs, and with me being locked-up, I wasn't much use to him. To be honest, if he's cheating, I don't mind, because Rashad is still a man with a very high sex-drive. I just wish he would write or visit me, so we could sort through our differences. I still loved my husband, and there was nothing I wouldn't do for my man. Today, I attempted to make another call to him, and just like the many times before, my call had been rejected.

"Shit!" I fumed as I slammed the phone down. I was steaming-mad because this has gotten ridiculous! I was now sick to my stomach because of him. I needed to know how he and my son been doing, but the bastard is making that a challenge.

"Can you move so I can use the phone now?" Rachel asked very rudely as she held her hand on her hip.

"I'm using it!" I said very sternly as I prayed she wouldn't say anything else.

"You been babysitting the phone for almost an hour now!" She huffed while she rolled her bug-eyes at me.

"And I plan on being on it for another hour!" I barked-back as I grabbed the phone and put it back to my ear.

"It's not that serious!" She warned as she huffed one last time before she walked away.

I couldn't believe how I was changing. Rachel had never done anything to me and here I was taking me frustration out on her. I needed Rashad to quickly-come to his senses before I pick-up another charge for killing someone. It's bad enough that I'm heartbroken and extremely-horny, but if I don't hear from Rashad soon, I don't know what I'd do!

****

Later that night, I was awoken by the rattle from the prison-guard's key as he entered the cell I shared with Rebecca. It was no secret, he was here to intercept Rebecca. I remained quiet as he shinned his light on Rebecca's bunk. I watched as she squinted her eyes before she had discovered it was Paul. Paul was a corrupt prison-guard that used his badge to gain sexual-favors from some of the inmates. And just like tonight, he was pulling Rebecca from her bunk to service him. I quickly closed my eyes once he shined his flashlight in my direction. I held my breath as I waited for them to leave. A

14

few seconds later, I heard the prison-bars close and sighed with relief. *(Thank God!)* I whispered to myself. I was relieved that Paul didn't have a change of heart. Truthfully, if Paul ever tried to make a move on me, he'd have to kill me, because I would definitely-kill him! The only man I ever been intimate with, was Rashad. He had taken my virginity. He had also made me promise that this will always be his pussy. Despite, the many times Rashad had cheated on me, that promise never been broken! I took a deep breath and said my prayers before I finally closed my eyes. I prayed that God protect me while I finish-out the last five-years of my sentence. I also prayed that Rashad and my son are in good-health, and that Rashad find the love he once had for me.

CHAPTER 3

After almost six long-months of fighting away unwanted dikes and shiesty ass prison guards, I finally received a letter from my best friend Stacey. I smiled as I quickly ripped open the letter that Stacey had sealed with a hot-pink kiss. I immediately smiled, because Stacey didn't change one bit, not even her favorite shade of lipstick. In the letter, she wrote...

"Dear Tia,

Hey girl!!! I'm so sorry I couldn't write you sooner. I had started a new job, and it requires a lot of my time. Anyways, I will be there to visit you next Wednesday. Until then... I love you and stay strong! Love, your bf Stacey."

I can't lie, Stacey's letter brought tears to my eyes. I was happier than I had been in a long time. I really missed her. Stacey and I go back since the third-grade. She had been more than a friend to me, she was my sister. Blood couldn't tell me shit, because the love I had for that girl made us family. She had been there for me many of times and over! One particular-time would be the day my mother died. She was the one that pulled me out of a severe case of depression when I just wanted to lay-over and die. We have laughed, and cried together. We shared many bittersweet memories. I was by her side when she fought and won her battle with cancer at just twenty-years old. Wherever she went, I went! When she fought, I fought! I had fought many of times, because Stacey's mouth was slick as silk. I didn't care if she was right or wrong, I had her back and she had mine. She was my Maid of Honor at my wedding. She's also my son's God mother. She had been looking-out for him since I'd been doing time. I just couldn't wait until next Wednesday so I could finally see my girl after almost a year. I smiled proudly as I got up and put her letter in a box with all the letters I'd gotten over the years. Every time I added a letter to my collection pile, it always made me proud to know that I was loved. Although, Rashad was on some other shit, I was happy to still have Stacey in my corner. I was feeling nothing but love right at this moment. I smiled as I climbed on my bunk and slowly closed my eyes.

*****

WEDNESDAY

Wednesday had finally come, and I was happy it did. I quickly rushed to the showers to freshen up for visitation. I was so happy when the guard had finally called my name.

"Tia King!" The Prison-guard shouted. I quickly brushed my edges back with my hand to make sure my hair was still in place. I refused to let Stacey see me looking bad. Although I'm in prison and severely-depressed because of Rashad, I wouldn't dare let that get in the way of looking my best for Stacey. Besides, Stacey was the definition of a stone-cold diva. She was very high maintenance and she only rocked the best, that consisted of Gucci and other designer labels. You can say she was what they called a designer junkie. As I walked-inside the visitation room, my smile was soon erased when I saw Stacey in her Gucci shades holding Rashad's hand, while leaning on his broad shoulders. This automatically made me feel uneasy. Then again, it may have been my insecurities caused by Rashad, because Stacey was my best friend and I know she would never hurt me. As I approached them, Stacey slowly-removed her shades, exposing her bright-blue contacts, while Rashad's eyes stayed glued to the floor.

"What's up Stacey, how you been girl?"

"Everything's been good," she nervously replied, as she looked over at Rashad while he continued to keep his head down.

"So, why are the both of yawl here?" I suspiciously asked while I watched as she continued to hold my husband's hand.

That's when Stacey took a deep breath and squeezed Rashad's hand even tighter while she looked deep-into my eyes.

"Tia, you know I love you, girl. But the real reason why we're both here...well... it's because," she said as she began to stutter.

"What is it? Has something happened to Junior?" I asked as I almost felt myself about to collapse.

"No, calm down... Junior is fine!" she assured me as I finally took a breath of relief.

"So, what is it then?" I asked as I impatiently waited for her to spit it out. I watched how Stacey began to clam-up and sweat while she wiped her forehead with her hand. Stacey had never been the type of person that's scared to speak her mind, so I knew whatever news she had for me, it had to be big.

After almost two-minutes of fondling over her words, Stacey took a long breath and finally responded.

"Rashad and I are engaged," Stacey shockingly revealed, as she boldly lifted her freshly manicured-hand, exposing a five-carat rock that drowned her anorexic finger.

"Excuse me?" I shouted, as I immediately became nauseated. I felt my head began to spin like a baller at a strip joint.

"I love you Tia, I really do! And I'm so sorry you had to find out like this. But Rashad and I are in love and we're going to get married. I hope that you can find it in your heart to be happy for us," Stacey revealed as she tried to apologize for her and Rashad's ultimate-betrayal. Before I knew it, I had grabbed a fist-full of Stacey's beautiful Brazilian-weave and yanked her scandalous-ass across the table that separated us.

"Calm down, Tia!" Rashad shouted, as he tried to pull me off her. At that moment, I truly lost it! I'd never felt this type of rage in my whole life. I wanted to kill that bitch! If it wasn't for the guards, I would have. I hit her with many more blows to her face, *repeatedly*. The guards struggled to pull-me off-of her.

"How dare you do me like this!" I bawled in rage as I cling to her neck before the prison-guards finally pulled me away. The visitation room became silent as visitors watched with their mouths hung-open in shock.

"I love you Rashad, why?" I demanded to know, while the guards continued to pull me out the visitation room.

"And Stacey, why? You were my best friend. You were my sister!" I shouted in the worst-pain as Stacey stared in silence while she wiped the blood from her bleeding-lip. Before the two-guards had finally pulled me out the visitation room, I told Stacey and Rashad something that they'll never forget.

"I'm only guilty of loving a man, so don't blame me for what I'll do for mine!"

Those were my last words before the guards finally hauled my ass to the box. I sat in the box mortified! I had so much hurt, anger, and sadness inside me. I couldn't believe the two-people I loved dearly would betray me like this. I felt like my life was over as I sat in the cold box. (*How did I let my life come to this? How did I let Rashad fool me?*) I thought as the icy-cold box made my body shiver. I soon had a flashback of that horrifying night that landed me here in the first-place. I'll never forget May 2nd, because that day I'd received a phone call from Nina, (Rashad's side-chick), the bitch that destroyed my life.

"Bitch! You said you need proof, well now you have it…You better come home quick!" she whispered as she breathed heavily into the phone before hanging up.

20

Nina and I had been communicating since I found her number inside Rashad's wallet when he was sleeping one night. I knew I should have left Rashad then, but I was so dumb and naïve. I just had to catch him in the act before my dumb-ass could believe it. I remember doing ninety on the highway and almost killing myself twice as I weaved in and out of traffic. I was determined to catch his lying, cheating ass, as I rushed home. I remember parking my car down the street at a neighbor's house as I quickly sprinted to the dream home, Rashad and I had just purchased.

My hands were shaking so badly as I reached in my purse for the keys to open my house door. I remember praying to God that the door didn't creek as I slowly pulled it open. I remembered how I slowly tiptoed through the house as I carefully made sure my stilettoes didn't click on our freshly-polished hardwood floors. I was out of breath when I had finally made it to my bedroom. My adrenaline was over the top, as I listened to heavy moans that were coming from behind my bedroom door. I slowly took a deep breath to calm myself before I turned the knob... The Good Lord just couldn't prepare me for what I was about to witness as I finally opened my room door...

"That's right! Eat this pussy!" this bitch moaned as my heart stopped when I saw my newlywed husband on his knees eating the hell out of Nina's nasty, unshaved-pussy. I watched in disgust as Rashad wiped her slimy-juices from his face when he saw he'd been caught. He was even bold-enough to try to explain why he had the bitches stank-pussy in his mouth. The fishy-smell mixed with Rashad's dishonesty made me nauseous, as I felt myself about to pass out. That's when Nina's ugly ass had the audacity to tell me she was pregnant. I felt my *world shatter as the hurtful-words escaped her bright-red lips. Everything that I worked hard for was about to go down the drain, including Rashad. I slowly pulled-out my Beretta and prayed it wasn't true, because I was also three-months pregnant. Rashad immediately began to deny her pregnancy, because he already knew I was about to kill him and her. Cheating was one thing, but to fuck this nasty-bitch without protection was war. And judging from the scent of hot-tuna fuming from between her legs, he better had said something very quick! Just like I predicted, Rashad immediately began to deny her pregnancy, but his side-bitch continued to push the issue.*

"You're a damn lie, Rashad! You know this is your baby!" she shouted as she quickly jumped up and put her finger in his face.

"Bitch, you're a damn lie! I would never fuck you raw, ever!" Rashad yelled back as he became very heated by her accusations.

"Are you kidding me, Rashad?" she shouted back, but this time her fists were balled as she stood toe-to-toe with him.

"You know exactly what I'm trying to say, bitch! That baby ain't mine!" he argued as he now balled his fists.

"Oh, so you're going to hit me now?" she questioned as she got even more offended by Rashad's lack of respect for her trifling ass.

"Man, just leave!" Rashad pleaded as he took a deep-breath to calm himself.

"I'm not going any fucking where. Not until you admit that I'm pregnant with your baby?" she demanded as she folded her arms and leaned on the side of her hip.

I watched in silence, but mostly I was traumatized. I couldn't believe Rashad's dirty secrets were unfolding right in front of me.

"No, that's not my baby! Now can you please leave?" Rashad begged, as he walked-over to our bedroom door and opened-it to escort her ass out. I guess that was the wrong move on Rashad's behalf, because that bitch went ballistic!

"You son of a bitch!" she shouted as she walked-up on him.

"You want to deny fucking me raw, but you just ate my pussy bare, right after Marlon oozed his gravy inside me, and it was thick gravy," she boasted with a proud smile on her face. I watched as Rashad's body went stiff while Nina continued to smile.

"Oh, and by the way… What his cum taste like?" she asked as she finally smirked as if she was saying checkmate.

By this time, my whole body was trembling, because I knew Rashad was about to fuck her up! He had a very bad temper and it was very clear she wasn't aware of that. After a moment of silence, Rashad had drawn back a pimp-hand that was blessed by the Gods on her ass. He hit that bitch so damn hard, I could have sworn he had broken her neck as she laid out on our bedroom floor. I watched with my mouth open as she miraculously got back up. I thought that would be her que to leave immediately. But instead, she slowly held the side of her face as she stumbled back to our king-sized bed and took a seat, knowing damn well her pussy reeked of hot fish.

"I'm not going anywhere," she calmly spoke as if she wasn't on the floor a second ago.

"Listen, it's not worth it!" I nervously spoke as I tried to beg her to go. I knew firsthand what Rashad was capable of, and murder was one. Nina just stared at me for a few-seconds before she slowly crosses her legs.

"I'm not going anywhere!" She boldly screamed as she looked-over at Rashad, who was trying his best to remain calm.

"Rashad, you're going to have to kill me, because I'm not going anywhere!" she demanded as she made herself more-comfortable as she slowly laid-out on our bed.

After telling her to leave about twenty-more times, Rashad had finally lost it. He had snatched Nina up by her braids and dragged her off our bed. As he tried to drag her out our bedroom, Nina grew angry. She immediately began kicking and biting his legs while she dug her long fingernails inside his skin.

"Get off me, bitch!" Rashad shouted in rage as he grabbed my Beretta from my hand and fired three-shots to Nina's head without thinking. I watched as her blood splattered everywhere! Nina's eyes were frozen wide-open, while her blood leaked from the bullet holes Rashad put in the back of her head. I couldn't believe my eyes when I saw her lifeless-body lying unconscious on our bedroom floor. Rashad and my eyes soon met in horror. We stood in silence for what seem like an eternity. After almost an hour of no-motion, we knew she was dead.

"Look what you made me do!" Rashad finally shouted, as he threw-down my gun and held-up his bloody-hands and began to panic. I couldn't believe he had the nerve to say it was my fault. He was the one that was caught cheating. Although it was my gun, he's the one that pulled the trigger, not me. After about thirty-minutes of playing the blame-game, we finally decided it was time to call the police. Rashad had no choice but to man up to what he'd done. (There was no way to cover this up, like last time), I thought to myself as I watched Nina's blood drip on our white carpet. I sat in silence as I watched how Rashad

nervously-pace the bedroom floor. Every two-minutes, he would place his head-on Nina's deceased-chest, in hopes of a heartbeat, but he got nothing. When the police finally arrived, reality soon hit me like Mike Tyson's fist.

(My husband can't go to jail!) My thoughts unleashed as Rashad slowly walked to the front door to let the police in. I quickly grabbed Rashad's t-shirt and wiped his finger prints off my gun. I just couldn't let my husband go down for murdering that bitch. He was right, it was my fault. If I would have never come home, none of this would've happened. It's only right that I take the charge for my man. Truth is, I love my husband more than I loved myself! The police followed Rashad to our bedroom and they soon discovered Nina's bloody corpse. Before the police could ask any questions, I immediately confessed.

"It was me!" I cried, as Rashad looked at me in disbelief. I inhaled my last breath as a free woman before I began to explain what happened to the police.

"I had come home early from work and caught Rashad cheating and I had snapped. I had pulled my gun from my purse, and I had shot her before she got to my front door. My husband tried to revive her, but it was too late, she was already gone," I cried as I kissed my future goodbye.

"Is that true?" the officers asked in disbelief as they both looked over at Rashad for confirmation. Rashad remain in silence for a few seconds before he nodded his head.

"Yes, it's true," Rashad shamefully said as I swallowed down the huge lump in my throat. I was immediately handcuffed and taken to jail. I sat in jail the whole time while I waited for my trial date. I ended up having my son in jail, while I awaited trial for a murder I didn't commit.

The sight of CPS taking my son freshly-out my womb was the most painful experience in my life. I thought I would die! Thank God for Rashad though, because he stepped right up and won custody of our son. I knew it was hard for Rashad to do, especially living the street life. But, as Rashad had promised, he refused to raise our son around drugs like he was. He immediately gave up the dope game to his favorite uncle on his daddy's side. He still received eighty percent from all dope profits. So, I knew my son would be financially straight, regardless! I even had Stacey crying her eyes out at my last visitation before I was finally sent up the road for murder.

"I promise, I'll look after Junior as if he is my own child," she promised me as we both shed tears as we said our goodbyes.

Exactly two weeks later, I was on the bus to do my ten-year sentence in prison. I remember how I sat in prison my first night, crying my eyes out, but I also knew it was for the best. I loved Rashad and the thought of him behind bars just made me sick. Somehow I still felt it was better me, than him. After I awaited trial for about a year, I was extremely blessed when the autopsy discovered that Nina was never pregnant. The grand jury found me guilty of voluntary-manslaughter. That sentence gave me the chance to see daylight again.

I now had five more years before I'm finally a free woman...

My attention was soon distracted by footsteps. I watched as my dinner-tray was pushed through the door by Tonya, while she wore a smirk on her face.

"You got five-minutes!" she shouted through the hole that separated me from whopping her ass. I watched as she pursed her lips together as if she was dying to say something to me.

"Whatever you have to say, just say it!" I finally spoke to break her awkward stares.

"All I have to say is nothing good comes out of sleeping with a dog, I don't care how good the dick is! You just better get-out before you catch fleas," she warned before she walked away.

I couldn't do anything but listen, because for the first time, I honestly believed she was right as I looked around the box that I was caged-in because of his punk ass.

"How could I be so damn naïve to have trusted them, though?" I whispered to myself, as I sat in the freezing box, trying to console myself from the hurt and blistering cold. I also thought about my son, and how I'd chosen a man over motherhood. I wanted to lay down and die. I felt like the whole world was against me, and there was nothing I could do about it. I just wished these five-years would soon come, so I could get back my life, my son, and my husband that was still rightfully mines.

CHAPTER 4

I'd been in the box for three long-months. I sat in that box in total isolation. Today, I had been released back to my cell. I can't lie, I was so happy to be back amongst other cell mates. Being in the box for three- months almost made me go insane! I also needed to vent, and the only people that could relate with me, were the people in my same shoes. As I vented to some of my cell mates, they all began to flood me with their opinions.

"I can't believe he did you like that!" Brandy said as she gently-rubbed my shoulders to console me. I quickly snatched away, because Brandy was a die-hard dike. She had been trying to turn me out since I first stepped foot in this prison, five years-ago. After telling her I wasn't gay over a thousand-times, she still decided to try and take it, just a like the punk-ass nigga she tried to be. Her and her dike friend T-red both tried to rape me in the showers. T-red held my arms while Brandy tried to go down on me. As soon as she got on her knees to taste me, I kneed her in her mouth, chipping her two front-teeth. Since that day, she never fucked with me again. I guess it's because of the constant reminder, every time she opened her mouth. Just last year, she had finally apologized and we been cool ever since. Peaches, Simone, and Big-Mary all had the same opinion though.

"Girl, you got to be crazy taking a charge for a nigga!" Big-Mary shook her head in disappointment. *Big Mary was the mother of the prison. She was as old-school as it gets. She reminded me of Big-Shirley from What's Happening. She rocked a big-afro with a zero-tolerance attitude. -And she always talked about the un-justice of our people. "Power to the people" was a saying she lived by. Unfortunately, she's currently serving a life-sentence for killing a crooked-cop that killed her only son, back in the seventies.*

"I know that's right!" Simone chimed-in as Peaches stared at me like I was insane. I wanted to be mad at them for calling-me crazy, but deep inside they were right. I was crazy and just plain-out stupid! I let my husband destroy my life and now he's engaged to my best friend, while I'm sitting behind bars. My therapy session was soon interrupted by the prison-guards, gave orders for everyone to return to their cells. As I stepped inside my cell, my cellmate Rebecca was already laying on her bunk, recovering from a "Jailhouse abortion" Big-Mary had performed on her. I slowly made my way to my highly uncomfortable bunk and laid down. Before I could close my eyes, Rebecca was whispering my name.

"What is it?" I finally answered very grumpily. I didn't mean to be snappy, but I was soaked in anger and feeling a severe case of a broken heart.

"I'm sorry to bother you, but I overheard you talking about your husband and best friend. Anyways, I just wanted to let you know that I personally know what you're going through… And if you ever need to talk, of course, you can find me right here," she said sarcastically, causing me to giggle.

"Thank you, Rebecca, that's very kind of you," I thanked her. I couldn't help but too often wonder why she was even here. Rebecca was a very preppy white-girl with natural blonde hair and sparkling-blue eyes. She was the Barbie of the prison. She has also become a "personal whore" for some of the guards and dikes on the campus. She had been passed around by many dikes and prison-guards in prison, but everyone knew her as Brandy's bitch. Brandy didn't play about her "snow bunny." That was the name Brandy had given her. But, as manly as Brandy appeared to be, that still didn't stop the male prison-guards from having their way with Rebecca. They would sneak her out her bunk late nights and once they were done, they'd sneak her back to her cell before any of the other guards noticed she was missing. She always come back with tears in her eyes and would always cry herself to sleep. She had been pregnant many times, but she would always go see Big-Mary for her famous, "Jailhouse abortion." Of course, no one ever mentioned the things that go down behind these prison walls. Those things become memories that we keep inside us, almost like a permanent stamp.

"Hey, can I ask you something?" I finally had the nerve to ask, because a lot of people prefer not to discuss the journey that landed them here.

"Yes, ask away," she said, very freely.

"Why are you in here?" I asked as I urgently waited for her to respond.

"I killed my husband and my maid of honor," she said very proudly.

"What?" I replied with an open-mouth.

"Yes, you heard me right," she proudly-smiled, but this time exposing her perfectly straight pearly white-teeth.

"What happened?" I impatiently asked as I longed to hear more.

"Let's just say they won't be able to laugh behind my back anymore!" she smiled wickedly as she laid back on her prison bunk.

I couldn't believe Rebecca was here for murder. She seemed so sweet and very humble. I guess even the sweetest person had a limit. It's just too bad, I didn't have one when it came to my husband. The fact remains, I love my husband and I'll fight to the end to win him back. Just then, I heard one of the female guard's yell...

"Lights out!" as all the lights went out in the compound. I laid on my bunk alone in the darkness. This was indeed going to be a long five-years, but for sake of my marriage, I had no choice, but to make it through. I slowly closed my eyes and drifted off to sleep.

CHAPTER 5

5 years Later

I couldn't believe it'd been five-years, as I slowly walked the prison floors for the last time. I was immediately greeted with cheers as I walked down the long hall that led to my freedom.

"We're going to miss you!" a lot of mixed voices shouted, as they hung on the bars that kept them caged like animals. I watched as Big-Mary silently shed tears as she tried her best to remain strong. Truth is, I was going to miss them, too. I had built a lot of friendships in the long ten-years I'd been here. I also learned a lot from these women, Big- Mary, Brandy, and especially Rebecca. It was very emotional saying goodbye to her. She was also a mother of two twin-boys. She longed to see her boys, but that would never be. Rebecca was in here for the long ride. She was in here on a life-sentence, without a chance of parole. She had made her husband and best friend suffer badly before she killed them. Their murders were so brutal, the jury had no pity for her, even if she looked like Malibu Barbie. Although, she had flatlined her husband and best friend, she had become a great friend to me. She really kept me sane these last five-years. I had witness a lot of suicides from women that just couldn't live with their life-sentences anymore. My eyes moistened when I thought about the many times I too, have contemplated suicide. If it wasn't for Rebecca's constant motivation and the thought of my son, I would have. Hearing her life stories made me want to fight harder for what I loved.

"Fight for love!!" Rebecca shouted as tears ran from her pretty blue eyes. I could also see the desperation in her eyes to be in my shoes. I just nodded my head, because it pained me to speak. I just know fighting is just what I intended to do.

As I walked outside the prison-door, the sunlight shined brightly in my face. I took in a deep breath as I smelled the sweet smell of freedom. I remembered walking in this prison at just twenty-four years old, but now I'm walking out as a fully grown middle-aged woman. I have physically changed, but the only thing that somehow remained the same, is the love I still have for Rashad.

I walked to the bus station in the same outdated clothing I wore exactly ten years-ago. I had so much on my mind, but picking-up where I left off was the only thing that held my interest. I finally made it to the bus station in the small town. The bus station looked abandoned, without a vehicle in sight. I slowly opened the door and found an old man sleeping at the counter.

"Excuse me sir," I whispered, making sure not to frighten him. After a few more attempts, the old man finally opened his eyes.

"Can I help you?" The old-man slowly replied.

"Yes, I need a bus ticket to Tampa, Florida."

"Tampa, Florida?" the old man strangely repeated.

"Yes, you heard correctly," I smiled, as the old man put his thick glasses on his face to get a better look at me.

"The last time we had a bus leave out of here for Tampa, Florida was about seven years-ago."

I knew right then the old-man had to be referring to my husband. Seven-years ago, he and my son moved here to be close to me and to also get away from anything that reminded Rashad of the street-life he was running from. After living here for only four-months, he said he couldn't find a decent job, so he and my son moved back to Tampa. He sold our brand-new 1999 CTS Cadillac, got a bus ticket and never looked back. I knew that was a lie, because the income he inherited from his family (*Drug*) business assured that he never had to work a day in his life. Now that I thought about it, I also recalled Stacey always saying she had to go out of town on business-trips every weekend. Now it's very clear, the business-trips she would always take had been right here with my husband. The many nights I would stay-up thinking about him, he was fucking my best friend. I couldn't even count the many times I begged him to come back, but he would always say that life in Tampa was much better than living in the backwoods of Georgia. Judging by the looks of this small town, he was right.

"I'm sorry, but the bus for Tampa comes tomorrow at noon," The old-man said with a frown on his face, as he gave me the bad news. I immediately felt my heart crush by the awful news.

"Are you sure?" I my voice cracked as I tried my hardest to fight back my tears that filled the web of my brown, exhausted eyes.

"I'm sorry huh, but that's the only time that bus will be available," he said with sorry eyes.

"Can you tell me where I can find the closet motel?" I dreadfully asked. Lord knows the last thing I wanted to ever do was spend another night in this God-awful town. I already gave this town ten-years of my life and I refused to give it another day.

"You're speaking nonsense!" The old man cheerfully-spoke as he looked at me with a big smile on his face. "There's a spare room right here," he excitedly pointed to a small room with a sofa bed inside.

"Are you sure?" I doubtfully asked, as I debated whether I should stay.

"Sure, it's fine," he smiled, as he escorted me to the small room.

"My wife made this room right for this special purpose. Matter of fact, she should be bringing me dinner very soon. If you like, it's plenty to go around?" he smiled very jollily as he rubbed his plumped belly. He reminded me of Santa Claus, which made me laugh.

"Yes, that will be fine," I smirked, as I watched him slowly walk out the door.

"Excuse me sir, will it be a problem if I borrowed your phone?" I asked with a desperate look on my face.

"Of course, not!" he grinned, as he quickly handed me his cellular phone.

I was so amazed by his cell phone. Technology had changed since the year 1999. This was my first time seeing a touch screen phone. After fumbling around with the old man's phone, I finally figured out how to use it. I quickly dialed Rashad's number. I was very surprised when a strange voice answered and said I had the wrong number.

"I can't believe he changed his number!" I shouted as I felt my anger rise. I quickly hung-up the phone and paced the floor, trying to calm myself. I soon dialed Stacey's number. I hadn't spoken to her since I pulled her across the table at visitation by her expensive weave. Although, I beat her ass at visitation, I remained very confident that she would still accept my call. I impatiently waited for her to pick up. To my surprise, she too had changed her number. I slowly ended the call and walked back to the front to hand the old man his phone. When I got to the front, his wife was standing at the counter with a lunch bag.

"You're just in time," the elderly man smiled as he took the lunch bag out his wife's hand. "I hope you like tuna sandwiches?" he warned, as he pulled out two sandwiches filled with tuna. The mention of tuna almost made me gag as I had a flashback of that horrifying day.

"Yes, tuna will be fine?" I sucked it up and graciously smiled as I took one of the tuna sandwiches from his hand. I had to admit, that was the best sandwich I'd eaten in ten long years. I slowly took small bites to savor the taste of the tuna that filled the sandwich. I didn't even realize the stares from him and his wife.

"I'm glad that you like it," His wife interrupted with a smile of appreciation on her round face. I was so embarrassed, as I quickly began to apologize for my bad eating manners.

"It's okay, we understand." They both smiled as if they already knew and I didn't have to say anymore.

After I ate my sandwich, I chatted with them for a while. I practically learned their whole life story. They even shared their love story of how they first met. Their story brought tears to my eyes. Although their families fought to keep them apart, their love for each other conquered all hate that tried to break them. They've now been together for thirty-eight years, with four children and six grandchildren. The way he looked at his wife as she told their story was so beautiful. He really loved his wife and the feeling was mutual. After talking to the beautiful couple for over an hour, I finally retired back into the spare room and laid on the sofa. I was so tired, I didn't bother to pull the bed from the sofa. I couldn't believe how comfortable the sofa felt, though. I guess it had something to do with laying on bricks for a decade. I yawned as I stretched my arms. I slowly closed my eyes and finally drifted off to sleep.

I was soon awoken by the skeletons from my past, as I laid drenched in my own sweat. "I thought I was done with these damn nightmares!" I whispered to myself, making sure not to wake the old man. I took a deep breath as I tried to block out the vison of crackhead Larry's face. It was as if God was reminding me of what Rashad and I had done, and although I prayed for forgiveness, I was still haunted as a reminder of my past.

"Dear God, please be merciful tonight! I'm sorry for what I done in the past, but please just give me one night of peace without waking up my skeletons that rest in my closet… Amen!" I prayed to God as I took a breath and closed back my eyes.

CHAPTER 6

The next day, I woke up to a knock at the door.

"Excuse me miss, your bus will be here in twenty minutes," The old man whispered from behind the door. I quickly jumped up and immediately began to panic. The thought of missing my bus, almost brought tears to my eyes. I just couldn't believe I had slept that long. I grabbed my bags and headed to the restroom to freshen up. I quickly made my way to the front of the bus station.

"There you are! I was in fear you'd miss your bus." he said as he looked down at his watch.

"I would have if it wasn't for you. Thank you!" I smiled as I thanked him.

"No problem. I'm just glad that I could help."

"Well, you have helped me a great deal, and I appreciate your hospitality," I assured him, as I watched him began to blush.

"You're quite welcome," he smiled as the bus had finally pulled up. "I don't expect to see you around here ever again!" he warned while he gave me a very stern look. He immediately reminded me of my father. Whenever I had done something wrong, mom would always have daddy to punish me. Dad could never find it in his heart to discipline me.

"I expect that you have learned your lesson, little girl!" he'd always say with a stern look on his face.

"Yes, daddy!" I would always respond as I held my head down, trying not to laugh.

"Good, next time I'm going to spank you!" he would always warn. Mom would be pissed when she found out daddy let my off the hook.

"That's why she's so spoiled now!" Mom would always oppose while daddy just smiled at me.

"What do you expect, she came from a woman that's sweet as sugar," he would always say. As hard as mom would try not to smile, dad would always win her over. That was one of daddy's gifts, he was very charming.

I immediately nodded my head in acceptance to his request, because there was no way I would ever let Rashad, or anyone, put me back in prison ever again!

"Just remember, life has its ups and downs. But, if you're up in the end, is all that matters," he smiled. As he finally opened the door, the light from the sun shined in my face. "Right on time, as always!" he smiled as he escorted me to the bus parked outside the station. My heart was filled with so much happiness as the old man walked me to the bus.

"Would it be a problem if I can have a hug?" I couldn't help but to request. Him and his wife had showed me such great hospitality that it would be a crime not hug him.

"Of-course!" the old man beamed as he opened his well-rounded arms to hug me.

"Thank you so much, and you will never see me again," I promised as I wiped my tears before they rolled down my cheeks.

"That's the best news I heard today," the old man whispered with an uplifting smile.

With nothing else left to say, I was on my way to Tampa, Florida, a place I called home. I was prepared and ready to fight for the family I'd left ten years-ago. I'd be damned if I let my trifling best friend Stacey take what's mine. On the way home, I thought about the good and the worst that could happen, but I didn't care. I'd been through the worst already. I had no other choice but to fight. I needed to fight for what was mine. Rashad and I shared secrets that no one else knew about, and I'd be damned if he left me after all I had done for him. I soon closed my eyes as I took a long nap to kill time. Besides, I needed all the rest I could get, because once I reached Tampa, Florida there would be hell to pay.

After riding the bus all night, I finally made it to Tampa. It was music to my ears when I heard the bus driver yell Tampa, Florida. I quickly grabbed my bag and exited off the bus. I took in a deep breath as I looked around. I couldn't believe I was here. Everything looked different from ten years-ago. There were new stores everywhere! Some of the old buildings had been renovated. This made me smile, because just like those old buildings that had been renovated, I too, could rebuild myself for the better and I planned to do just that. I was exactly twenty minutes away from my beautiful home, and the life I had once abandoned. I didn't waste any time as I quickly called a cab.

About ten minutes later, the Yellow Cab pulled up. I quickly got in and gave the cab driver the address that I shared with my husband, Rashad. On the ride home, I had developed a sick feeling about coming home unannounced. But, honestly, I didn't give a damn. Last I checked, both our names were on the mortgage and I put up some money on the house, too. As I approached my neighborhood, I noticed a lot had changed. The neighborhood was now filled with plenty of homes. When Rashad and I purchased our home over ten years ago, there was no more than three homes on the lot. Everything looked deserted. Rashad would always joke and say, "It's a good thing, because no one will ever hear you scream from all the love we'll make."

And he wasn't lying, we fucked everywhere! The orgasms Rashad had given me were so mind-blowing, I would lose my damn mind! I would scream out some of the most unusual things. The next morning, Rashad would always tease me about what I had said while we were having sex.

"You better be happy we don't have neighbors yet, because what you said last night would have forced them to put a for sale sign on their home," he'd always joke.

It's just too bad that ten years had passed since Rashad and I had sex in our home. As the cab driver pulled into my driveway, I noticed the yard was well landscaped with beautiful flowers. There were also two brand-new pearly white

Jags parked in the driveway. I quickly handed the cab driver twenty dollars and grabbed my bag as I exited the vehicle. My heart was pounding as I made my way to the front door. I couldn't control my trembling hands as I reached in my bag and pulled out the same set of house keys that put me in this situation in the first place. I held the key steady with both hands as I tried to open the door. My worst nightmare had been confirmed. I couldn't open my front door with my key.

"I can't believe Rashad has changed the locks," I whispered as I tried a couple more attempts to open the front door. *(Just keep calm),* I said to myself as I slowly rang the doorbell.

A few seconds later, A young boy finally opened the front door. I couldn't believe my eyes when I realized it was my very own son. He had grown so much, and he was so handsome! He was a perfect mixture of me and Rashad. The last time I saw my son was eight-years ago, when he was just three-years old. Rashad decided it was no longer appropriate for him to see me in prison. I agreed, but I'd write him every single day. That was, until Rashad had stop accepting letters from me.

"Can I help you, ma'am?" the little boy politely asked, as he looked at me very suspiciously.

"Junior… it's me, I'm your mother!" I cried joyfully as I wrapped my arms around my son. I was soon crushed when Junior pushed me away.

"I'm sorry, but my mother's dead!" he said frightened, as he yelled for his daddy to come quick. I felt a huge blow to my chest. I couldn't believe Rashad would tell our son that I was dead. Just then, Rashad came running down the stairs. He looked like he'd seen a ghost when he laid eyes on me.

"What are you doing here!" Rashad shouted as if he'd saw a ghost.

"You told our son I was dead!" I furiously shouted, as I felt the worst kind of pain in my life.

"Go to your room, Junior!" Rashad demanded, while Junior looked confused. "Go now!" Rashad screamed again, causing Junior to jump as he ran upstairs to his room.

"What the hell are you doing here?" Rashad immediately began to confront me.

"Excuse me, did you think I'd be in there forever?" I asked, as I felt disrespected by Rashad's lack of happiness to see me.

"I know that, but what are you doing here?" he asked as if he was appalled that I would be at my own doorstep.

"I live here, Rashad!" I shouted back as I looked at him like he'd gone crazy.

"Not anymore!" he said in a disgusting tone as he tried to close the door.

"What do you mean, not anymore?" I retaliated as I swiftly stopped the door with my foot. I soon found it very hard for me to catch my breath.

"You haven't lived here in over ten-years. Why in the hell would you think this is still your house?" Rashad questioned as he looked at me like I was crazy.

"That's because I've been locked up, remember!" I hollered on the top of my lungs, as I couldn't believe how ungrateful Rashad had become.

"You don't have to keep reminding me. I know you've been locked-up, because I'm the one that's been making sure your commissary was full, remember!" he said very sarcastically.

Just then there were loud footsteps coming down the stairs. I was surprised when I realized it was Stacey, as she placed her tiny hands on her petite hips.

"What the hell is she doing here, Rashad!" Stacey squealed.

"Excuse me, what am I doing here? I live here, what the hell are you doing here?" I steamed as I felt the heat from hell enter my soul as I prepared myself for a showdown.

"Negative! You used to live here," Rashad interrupted, as Stacey began to smirk.

"This is my house!" I now bawled, as tears streamed from my eyes. I was so hurt by Rashad's rude behavior towards me. I thought he'd have better respect for the woman that risked her life to save his.

"Listen, we are even! I've been taking care of our son, and been putting money inside your commissary. I haven't asked you to repay a dime, have I! Now you want to show up on my damn doorstep like you running shit?" Rashad snarled as his body buffed-up.

"That has nothing to do with this. This is my home too, Rashad!" I bristled as I pushed my way inside the French doors of the home I hadn't entered in over a decade.

"Get out!" Stacey immediately yelled, as she tries to push me back out the door. I guess with all the commotion going on, it brought our son back downstairs.

"Daddy, what's going on?" Junior screamed-out in fear.

"Nothing son, everything is okay. I want you to go back to your room," Rashad demanded while he tried to close the door.

"No! I'm your mother and you don't have to go anywhere!" I barked as I pushed through the door and reached out my hand for him to join me downstairs.

"She is not your mother Junior, I am!" Stacey had the audacity to say.

I had lost it at that very second, as I grabbed Stacey by her weave and slammed her to the floor.

"I'll kill you, bitch!" I screeched as I wrapped my hands around her ostrich-neck and tried to choke the dear life out her body.

"Let go of her!" Rashad interfered as he tried to pull me off her. I guess my anger had out-strengthened his power, because Rashad couldn't move my ass! I had lost it, as I saw Stacey's eyes rolling in the back of her head.

"Mom stop!" I soon heard the voice of my son yell.

There was something in my son's voice that overpowered all the anger I was feeling. Just to hear him call me mom after so many years was the most amazing feeling in the world. His voice alone gave me the courage to release Stacey's neck. I quickly got up and slowly walked up the steps to hug my son. As I got to the last step, I was now standing face-to-face with my son. The look on his face was very calm. His eyes were full of wonder, as if they were asking where I'd been? I slowly extended my arms to grab his hand. I hadn't felt the flesh of my son's hand in eight long years. I missed my son tremendously! As I grabbed for his hand, I felt my head being yanked back as if my neck would break at any second. As I turned around, I noticed it was Rashad holding a fist full of my hair. Before I could respond, he had pulled me down the stairs by my hair.

"Get the fuck out of my home!" he proclaimed as he pulled me right out the door. I was so distraught by Rashad's actions, I just laid on the front porch, bawling my eyes out.

"Why Rashad, why!" I screamed with so many emotions. The main emotion I identified myself with, was anger. I had given that nigga so much of me, and now he's trying to take the very last bit of me, by taking my son?

"Open the fuckin door, Rashad!" I viciously screamed as I pounded my fist on the front door. "Please! Just open the door, I just want to see my son!" I begged and begged, but still my pleas and knocks were ignored.

After banging on the door for almost an hour, I finally pulled myself together. By this time, all the neighbors were on their front porch watching me make a complete fool of myself, but I didn't care. I'd made plenty fools of myself in the past, but this was my last chance at life and if it meant camping out on my front lawn, I'd do so. And I did just that.

I quickly pulled the small blanket out of my bag and spread it on the concrete by the doorway. I had made up my mind. I wasn't going anywhere! I'd been gone from my home for too long and it would be a cold day in hell before I go another day, away from my home. I folded myself into a ball, as I wrapped my jacket around me to shield out the cold breeze. This immediately reminded me of the time I had found my mother inside her closet, wrapped into a ball, as she quietly cried in pain.

She had just discovered she contracted AIDS from Dad's infidelities. I remember how I wrapped my arms around her and told her everything would be okay. Back then, I didn't know how serious AIDS really was. I distinctively remember the smile my mother gave me, because her smile showed so much warmth and beauty. Although, her eyes were filled with so much pain, she could somehow smile through her pain, and her smile was so angelic! Just to think of how strong my mother was, had now given me strength. I soon took in a deep breath and through the vast pain I was feeling, I slowly smiled. I had realized, *"No matter what I've been through, or am going through… anything was better than the bullshit my daddy put my mother through.*" I assured myself. I slowly wiped my tears from my face and smiled before I gently closed my eyes, and drifted off to sleep.

CHAPTER 7

I was soon awakened by a bright-flashlight as it shined in my face.

"Ma'am, get up!" a male's voice said very sternly as he continued to shined his flashlight right into my face. I squinted my eyes and realized it was two police-officers, joined by Stacey and Rashad. I slowly got up, and looked over at the officers and Rashad.

"Ma'am, why are you sleeping outside?" the male officers curiously asked.

"My husband kicked me out," I shamefully mumbled, because the words were so painful to reveal. The female officer seemed stunned to hear the shocking truth.

"Excuse me, come again?" she asked, as Rashad shamefully put his head down like he always did.

"She's about to be my ex-wife!" he blurted out. I guess he felt that ex, would have made the situation less shameful.

"I'm not understanding. I need someone to explain what's going on?" the female officer responded as she glanced at the three of us for answers.

"Sure officer, I would love to explain!" I smirked, because I knew she would love to hear this backwoods drama we had going on. I quickly cleared my throat as I began to explain…

"Well, after doing ten-years for my ungrateful husband, I found out that he gotten engaged to my best friend, although we're still married. He stopped accepting my phone calls and letters when I was in prison. Well, today I've come home after ten long years to realize that the locks on our doors have been changed, and that my husband has moved my ex-best friend into our home and been raising my son to believe I was dead."

The looks on both the officers' faces were priceless.

"Now, I have nowhere to go. So, that's why you see me sleeping outside," I explained while I dropped my head in shame.

"Is this true?" The male officer asked Rashad with a look of disgust.

"It's not like that!" Rashad immediately tried to explain his side of the story.

"Is your wife on the mortgage, yes or no?" the female officer sternly interrupted. I could tell by her tone of voice she was very pissed at Rashad.

"Well technically, she is, but I'm...." Rashad tried to explain as he fumbled for an excuse.

"There's nothing else you can say. If she's on the mortgage than this is just as much her home as yours," the female officer quickly explained. Rashad's face looked like he'd seen a ghost, while Stacey stared in horror.

"But we are getting married in a few months," Stacey immediately tried to add her two cents.

"Well that's fine, but until their divorce is final and they have come to an agreement, this is still their home!" she explained as she looked at Stacey like some filthy homewrecker.

"And besides, if he could do his own wife like this, then maybe you ought to reconsider," the male officer chimed in as he winked over at Stacey while escorting me back inside my home. I was so happy to feel the warm heat as my body began to thaw out from being in forty-degree weather.

"I'm expecting no more problems, because I'd really hate to come back, right?" the male officer said, as he looked directly over at Rashad.

Rashad just nodded his head while Stacey stormed upstairs to the bedroom that once belong to me and slam the door. I thanked the police officers as I quickly closed the door. After the police left, I locked the door and smiled. I couldn't believe I was finally home. I didn't waste any time as I headed straight to my son's room. I watched as he slept. He was so handsome! I couldn't believe I was so damn stupid to give him up for Rashad's selfish ass. I slowly bent down and kissed him gently on his cheek.

I was now home and nothing was going to stop me this time from being a mother. After watching my son sleep, I slowly walked down the hallway that lead to what used to be mine's and Rashad's bedroom. Although, I was hurt and full of anger, I didn't want to start anymore trouble for tonight. I just needed a pair of my old pajamas, because I had nothing but the clothes on my back. I gently knocked on the bedroom door, as I waited for someone to answer. After waiting for about ten minutes, Rashad had finally opened the door.

"What!" he shouted in a very hateful tone.

"I didn't come to start any drama, I just need a pair of my old pajamas and I'll be out your way," I said as pleasant as I possibly could. Rashad stared at me for a moment, before he walked off. A few seconds later, he returned with my red lace nightgown.

"Thank you!" I smiled, as I remembered this was Rashad's favorite nightgown he'd love to see me in.

I quickly retired to the bathroom where I took a long hot bath. I closed my eyes as I thought of a strategy to win my husband back. After soaking in the tub for about an hour, I dried off and slipped on my night gown. I was surprised how my body had change in ten years. I was all woman and there was no denying that. My bobs spilled through the top, while my booty and hips filled my night gown like a glove. I no longer had my boyish figure. I was rocking the meanest hour glass figure ever built. I looked very sinful in my sexy red nightgown. Just the look of me inside my gown had turned me on.

The only vision I had in mind was of Rashad taking it off me. I slowly walked downstairs to the living room, and laid on the cold leather couch. I loved how the leather cooled my scorching hot body. I tried to close my eyes and just enjoy the feeling of being home, but I couldn't. The only thing I could think about was my husband being laid up with my best friend while I laid downstairs on the sofa. I found myself searching through my old movie collections to take my mind off Stacey and Rashad. I came across my old wedding video. I smiled wickedly as I popped it in. I watched as I slowly walked down the aisle to *You,* by Jesse Powell. I was so young and so in love. The look on Rashad's face showed the same emotion, and that was love. I watched as we exchanged vows, and how we passionately kissed as the pastor announced us husband and wife.

As I watched my wedding video, tears poured down my face. I wouldn't believe in a million years that our beautiful union would fall to the slums of hell. Then to add fuel to the fire, I watched my Maid of Honor, my best friend Stacey, smiling as she gives a toast and wishes us all the happiness in the world. This made my blood boil! How could she wish us all the happiness in the world when she's lying upstairs with my husband? I wanted to grab the butcher knife in the kitchen and slaughter them both, but I refused to leave my son again. They weren't worth it!

As I wiped my face, I heard footsteps coming down the stairs. I was shocked when I realized it was Rashad. He quickly glimpsed at me and our wedding video I had playing as he quickly walked to the kitchen. I watched as he poured himself a glass of water. I knew he had to have just finished fucking Stacey's guts out, because after sex, he'd always drink a glass of water. I just kept my head straight as I continued to watch our wedding video. I wished I could crawl inside the television screen and relive that special day. Just as I was reminiscing on our special day, Rashad stood in front of the TV, making sure to block our wedding video.

"What is it, Rashad?" I asked as I held my head down.

"I just want to say I'm sorry. I know it doesn't mean shit now, but I'm sorry," he said as he stared at me as if he was waiting for me to accept his apology. I just stood in silence as if I didn't hear him.

"Tia, I never wanted to hurt you like this. You are a good woman and any man would love to have you," he said very quietly so Stacey wouldn't be able to hear.

"But I want you, Rashad!" I quickly blurted out as I broke down and cried. "Why can't I just have you, baby?" I begged as I slowly got off the sofa and walked in front of him.

I wanted Rashad so bad I could taste him! I guess Rashad could feel the intense passion I had for him. He slowly stared in my eyes for a few seconds, before he slowly pulled me into him. Just his touch and body heat drove me insane.

"Shh!" he whispered as he gently rubbed his hands over my aching body. My heart was pounding so hard you could hear it through my night gown. This is what I'd been waiting ten years for.

"Please baby, make my pain go away," I begged as I my body began to shiver.

It was like Rashad was a powerful drug. Although he was bad for me, I'd risk my life to have him. Just then, Rashad pulled me tighter inside his ripped arms and held me. The smell of his cologne almost made me orgasm. He smelled so damn good! I felt the gentle touch of his hands as he began to rub my thighs.

"Look at me," I demanded as tears ran down my eyes. I wanted him to see every emotion he created. Rashad stared in my eyes as I requested, as he slowly worked his way to vagina. I was already soaking wet. Just as he placed his hand on my special place, everything was soon interrupted by Stacey's squeaky voice as she screamed for Rashad.

"Don't go, please!" I begged Rashad as I gripped his t-shirt. Rashad looked like he wanted to stay, but something about Stacey just outpowered me. I watched, defeated, as my husband walked back upstairs to join her. I was so hurt and frustrated, I punched the wall with my fist. I then ran to the sofa where I buried my face inside the throw pillow. My first night home was ruined. I cried my eyes out before I finally fell asleep.

CHAPTER 8

The next morning, I woke up to the sound of dishes being thrown in the sink. I opened my eyes to realize it was Stacey, preparing breakfast.

"Hurry up, Junior! You don't want to be late," she shouted upstairs. This made me pissed as I quickly jumped up. I refused to let her fix my son breakfast. It was bad enough she has taken my husband, but I'd be damn if she takes my son too.

"No! That's okay, I'll make him breakfast." I quickly interrupted, as I headed straight to the kitchen. Stacey's eyes almost hit the floor when she saw what I was wearing. She quickly rolled her eyes and stormed upstairs. Five minutes later, Junior made his way downstairs.

"Hey baby! What can I fix you for breakfast?" I proudly asked.

"Where's Stacey?" he immediately asked as he looked confused as to why I was in the kitchen.

"Stacey is busy. I'll be making you breakfast from now on. I'll make anything you want!" I assured him with a smile.

"Okay, can I have pancakes?" he asked with a little smirk on his face. He had the same smile and left dimple as Rashad, which I thought was very cute.

"Yes, of course!" I smiled, as I happily prepared his pancakes.

About ten minutes later, Stacey returned. She seemed aggravated when she discovered I had made Junior pancakes.

"Junior! You know I said no pancakes!" she bristled like an animal waiting to attack.

"Excuse me, don't you ever yell at my son again! I became indignant as Junior stared nervously. I quickly calmed myself before I ignite into a cat fight with her ass.

"I said it was okay for him to have pancakes," I explained as calm as possible, but deep inside I was praying for Stacey to step-out of line. My anger had vanished as I looked over at Junior who was now sporting the biggest smile on his face.

Stacey quickly grabbed her purse and stormed out the door, slamming it behind her. After Junior finished eating, he asked if I could walk him to his bus stop.

"Of course, I will!" I beamed, as ran upstairs to get dress. When I returned, he quickly grabbed his book bag and was ready to go.

We talked as we walked down the street to his bus stop. Some of the parents at the bus stop were looking funny when they saw me, instead of Stacey. A few were even whispering, but I didn't care. All I know is, I was happy! I felt so proud when Junior yelled bye mom as he got on the bus. I quickly sprinted home with a big smile on my face. I hadn't smiled like this in a long time.

Once I made it home, I did all the household chores. The house looked and smelled very clean. I knew that I would finally get some recognition from Rashad, seeing that Stacey couldn't clean for shit! After cleaning, I got dressed and caught a cab to the local library. I was determined to get my life back. After doing some research for a couple hours, I decided to pick up a few groceries to make Junior some spaghetti for dinner tonight. He told me it was his favorite food. I quickly retrieved the items I needed to prepare his spaghetti dinner. After I finished grocery shopping, I called a cab and was on my way back home. When I arrived home, I noticed Stacey's car parked inside the driveway. I couldn't help but to smirk as I walked inside the door. Stacey looked like she'd seen a ghost. I didn't bother to pay her any mind as I walked straight to the kitchen to put the groceries down. After I put the groceries down, I went straight to my son's bedroom. He was so busy playing his video game he didn't notice I was standing behind him.

"Hey son!" I finally interrupted.

"Hey mom!" he quickly replied as he continued to play on his Xbox.

"I'm making spaghetti!" I said proudly as I waited for his response.

"That's great mom, spaghetti is my favorite!" he smiled as he licked his lips.

"I know!" I smiled, as I watched how big he had grown. "Do you have homework?" I proudly asked, because it felt so good to finally play the role of a mother.

"I've done it already," He smiled as he continued to pound away at his controller.

"Okay, that's great! Do you need me to check it?" I smiled, as I looked forward to checking my son's homework for the first time.

"No, Stacey already checked it," he said as he turned back around and continued to play his video game.

I felt crushed that Stacey would overstep her boundaries. It was different when I was gone and now that I'm back, I would love for her to acknowledge my presence. Junior was my son and it's time that I took on the parenting role of his mother.

"Okay, well I'm about to start dinner. You have one hour then I need you to wash up for dinner, okay?"

"Yes, mom." Junior said with the cutest pout. I just smiled as I exited his bedroom. As I walked down stairs, I saw Stacey in the kitchen. I couldn't believe she was boiling hotdogs for dinner. I quickly made my way inside the kitchen to prepare my spaghetti dinner. (*It will be a cold-day in hell before my son ate hotdogs for dinner*), I thought to myself.

The kitchen was so quiet you could hear a pin drop, but I preferred it this way. Stacey had once meant so much to me. There was a time when I would have given her the clothes off my back, but now I wouldn't even piss on her if she was engulfed in flames. I hated her, and judging by the awkward silence, the feeling was mutual.

Thirty minutes later, the front door opened and in came Rashad. Rashad was dripping sweat and his work clothes were very dirty. In some weird way, it had turned me on. I always had a fetish for construction workers. I was also happy to see him making an honest living, and most of all, he had kept his promised. He had promised me that when our son was born, he would get out the dope game. Although, it was hard for him, he did just that.

Rashad was born into the dope game. His mother and father sold every drug you can name. They had Tampa and the whole state of Florida on lock. When I first met Rashad many years back, he was iced out, and his rides was clean. He'd always come through the drive-thru blasting his music and smelling like pounds of weed. I didn't like that one bit, because I would always have to scream at the top of my lungs to take his order. Stacey would always put extra food inside his bag. I've should have known right then that she was crushing over Rashad. But then again, she always was giving away free food to every man that came through the drive-thru. That's exactly why she got fired. My thoughts were soon interrupted when Stacey ran and greeted my husband with a long passionate kiss.

"I missed you baby," she smiled as she glanced back at me. I knew she was just putting on to make me jealous, but little did she know, I was about to get the last laugh. It was very clear that her mammy didn't teach her that the way to a man's heart is through his stomach.

"Damn! It smells good in here. What you cookin', baby?" Rashad asked as he sniffed around the kitchen like a blood hound. Stacey's mouth dropped as she held her head down.

"I made hotdogs," she finally mumbled in shame.

"Junior, dinner is ready!" I shouted, as I pilled Junior's plate with spaghetti, salad, and homemade garlic bread.

Rashad's face dropped, causing me to smirk as I proudly brought my and Junior's plates to the dinner table. Junior ran downstairs like lightning and quickly took a seat at the table. Junior didn't waste any time stuffing his face with spaghetti.

"Umm! This is good!" Junior said with delight.

"Thank you, baby, and it's plenty more delicious meals where that came from," I smiled as I looked back at Stacey. The look on her face was priceless! She quickly marched upstairs with Rashad right on her tail.

After dinner, Junior and I retired to his bedroom where he taught me how to play his Xbox. He smiled proudly to know his mommy was a fast learner.

"Mom, you are good!" he bragged. "I tried to teach Stacey, but she still can't play," he whispered, causing me to laugh.

My son was very respectful and he cared about others, that was something he clearly inherited from me. After playing the Xbox, we talked about school and all the things he liked to do. I just couldn't believe we had bonded so well. We talked so much, I didn't realize it was his bed time, until Rashad came to the door.

"Junior, it's time for bed," he shouted as he waited by the door.

"Okay daddy," Junior mumbled as he pouted.

Before he jumped in bed, he ran into my arms and gave me the tightest hug I'd ever felt. It was like he had hugged my soul and I didn't want to let him go. I glimpsed over at Rashad as he watched from the bedroom door. The love we had was unbelievable. I watched as Rashad soon left the room, I think it had something to do with the guilt he felt. I slowly tucked my son in. I wanted to savor every moment. I watched as he closed his eyes. As I hit the light switch to leave, my son said something I wasn't prepared for.

"Mom, why did you leave me?" he whispered, causing my heart to drop from my chest. I quickly ran to his bedside and held his precious hand.

"Junior, what I did is something that can never be explained," I said as I stared at him in the darkness. "Just know I did what I did for you," I whispered, as I wiped the tears from my burning eyes. The room was quiet for a few seconds before Junior responded. "Can you promise not to leave me anymore?" he said in a voice that almost torn me apart.

"I promise that I'll take a trip to hell before I ever leave you again!" I assured him as I tightly gripped his hand. I then kissed his cheek and finally exited his room.

As I walked down the hallway, I noticed all my belongings were packed in bags outside of my old bedroom door. I didn't bother to make a scene. I just grabbed the bags and put them inside our guest bedroom which had now became my new bedroom. I quickly pulled out all my clothing inside the bag. I couldn't believe all the nice things I owned. It's just too bad that my clothing is now outdated, but it would have to do for now. I found some more of my old night gowns. I discovered that every night gown I owned were all very sexy and revealing. I didn't have any cotton gowns if it was to save my life. I guess it had something to do with being a newlywed at the time.

My mother would always say, *"The last image your husband should always see before he closes his eyes at night, is the look of his beautiful wife in lingerie."* My mom swore by that quote, and since mothers are always right, I bought nothing but the sexiest lingerie. I quickly picked up my black silk night gown and retired to the bathroom. After my bath, I went downstairs for a cup of tea. As I walked downstairs, I noticed a lot of noise coming from the kitchen. I was surprise to discover Rashad at the kitchen table stuffing his face with the left overs I'd cooked for dinner. He looked like a deer caught in headlights.

"Tia, I can explain," he quickly responded as he wiped the spaghetti sauce from his mouth.

"It's okay Rashad, I understand," I smiled as I continued to make some tea. We stood in silence for about five minutes before Rashad responded.

"Listen Tia, I noticed you've been catching the cab and I feel that isn't right," he explained as he held his head in shame.

I couldn't believe my ears as I heard Rashad finally address things that weren't right. It's just too bad he couldn't admit that trying to marry my best friend was amongst the worst!

"Anyway, I decided you should use my car until I buy you a car of your own," he said as he finally looked up at me.

"But how are you going to get to work?" I asked as I somehow managed to put his needs before mine, again.

"Don't worry about that," he quickly assured as he finished off the last bit of his spaghetti and got up to leave.

"Oh, and about the spaghetti thing, I'd appreciate if you kept this between us," he whispered as he looked back to see if the coast was clear.

"Of course," I smiled as I sipped on my peppermint tea. I felt so good inside, because slowly but surely, I was winning my husband back.

CHAPTER 9

The next day, as promised, there was a knock at my bedroom door. I quickly got out of the guest bed and opened the room door. Standing at the door was Rashad with his car key at hand.

"Be careful!" was his only words as he handed me the keys to his brand new 2010 Jag and walked away.

I quickly looked down the hallway, where I saw Stacey with the long face. It looked like she smelled ten pounds of uncleaned chitterlings as she followed Rashad downstairs. I smiled as I quickly got dressed. I squeezed on a pair of my old blue jeans and white tank top. I combed my long black hair that reached the middle of my back. That was one good thing I could say about being in prison for ten years, it had grown the hell out of my hair and nails. My skin was also flawless, and I looked beautiful! I quickly walked downstairs where my son was waiting at the breakfast table for his breakfast.

"Morning, sweetie!" I smiled. I couldn't help but to notice how much my son resembled me.

"Morning, mom," he said as he laid his head on the table. "What's wrong, son?" I asked concernedly as I took a seat next to him.

"Dad promised he'd get me Dead Redemption," he said with a pout on his face.

"Is that why you have the long face?" I asked as I stroked his back to console him. "I tell you what, let's get you some breakfast and we'll talk about this afterwards. Okay?" I smiled as I gently rubbed his back.

Finally, Junior had cheered up and politely asked me for some Captain Crunch cereal. I poured him a big bowl and smiled. After eating, I walked him to his bus stop where we talked some more. After his bus came, I quickly headed back home. I was determined to get that game for my son. I ran upstairs and counted the money I had left from working in prison. I only had a $150.00 left to my name and I refused to ask Rashad for a dime. I grabbed Rashad's car keys and headed to the blood bank to sale my blood. I received $50.00 dollars for my blood.

I headed to Game Stop, where I purchased the video game for my son. I was so happy and very proud of myself. On my way home, I stopped by the grocery store and picked up some ingredients to make my famous mac-n-cheese. I knew it was Rashad's favorite. When I got home, I wrapped Junior's present, placed it on his bed, and went to prepare dinner. I had just taken my homemade mac-n-cheese out of the oven when Stacey, Rashad, and Junior walked through the door.

"Umm! It smells good in here, don't it daddy?" Junior said happily as he made his way inside the kitchen.

"Yes, it does smell good son," Rashad smiled, as Stacey rolled her fake blue eyes she'd been rocking since 1998.

"Go put your book bag down so you can eat," I smiled as Junior quickly ran to his room. A few seconds later, there was a big scream as Junior ran down the stairs.

"Thank you! Thank you, thank you daddy, you're the best!" Junior shouted as he tightly hugged his daddy's neck while Rashad looked very confused.

"Why are you hugging me?" he finally asked as he looked at Junior very strangely.

"Because you're the best dad in world!" he shouted as he held up his brand-new video game. Rashad immediately looked over at me. I quickly gave him a wink to signal him to go along with it.

"Thanks son, and you're welcome," he said with a puzzled look on his face.

"I thought you said you weren't getting him that damn game!" Stacey shouted as she stormed upstairs. Rashad gave me a quick look, before he ran after Stacey.

I didn't care about whatever drama Stacey had going on, because I was very happy that my son was happy. I made me and Junior a plate. I even secretly made Rashad a plate, wrapped it up, and placed it in the refrigerator. I knew he would sneak down to eat it later tonight. After dinner, I played the brand-new video game with my son until it was time for him to go to bed. I gave him a good night kiss and closed his room door. I quickly grabbed my night gown and headed for the bathroom. After my bubble bath, I went to the kitchen to fix my nightly tea. Like before, Rashad was sitting at the table eating the food I'd left for him. We smiled as our eyes made contact. It was almost like a little secret only we shared. As I made my tea, I felt Rashad standing behind me as he breathed down my neck. I immediately closed my eyes as I enjoyed the heat from his breath.

"That was a nice thing you did for Junior," he whispered in my ear.

Thank you," I mumbled, as I became flushed from being so close to the man I loved unconditionally.

"But why did you give me the credit?" he asked as he lifted my arm, exposing the bandage that covered my bleeding vein. I was so caught up with making today perfect, I had forgot to remove the bandage from my arm. I took in a deep breath before I finally responded.

"I knew he would appreciate it more if he knew it came from you," I whispered, as my heart beat intensely.

"I know you did," he whispered back as he gently wrapped his arms around my waist.

"Rashad don't," I whispered as I closed my eyes. I knew Rashad was bad for me, but for some reason, I always decide to take the risk.

"Don't do what?" he asked as he slowly slipped his hand up my night gown.

"Please, Rashad!" I begged, as a lake grew between my legs. I wanted him so bad, but I was terrified of being hurt again. Rashad ignored my plea as he gently kissed my neck, causing my juices to drip down my thighs.

"Oh God, Baby!" I cried as Rashad slowly pulled my night gown up and bent me across the kitchen sink. I closed my eyes as he removed my panties with his teeth. After he pulled them to my ankles he softly planted kisses to my vagina that became his personal drinking well. I moaned very softly, in fear that this moment would be ruined if Stacey interrupted us. My manners were soon gone once I felt Rashad's warm, wet tongue flickered the inside of my vagina.

"Oh God! Baby!!" I moaned loudly, as Rashad continued licking my soul from between my legs. "What are you doing to me?" I cried, as I felt all my feelings escape from my lips.

"I'm giving you what you want," he said, as he pulled down his pants exposing his beautiful, smooth chocolate dick.

I immediately began to twitch as I'd been impatiently waiting for him to bless me with some of his black magic. He did just that, as he forced it deeply inside of me. I literally felt every inch of his massive steel. I was so tight from being five years overdue. The last time Rashad and I had sex was six years ago, but it was always very quick, due to the hour visit. This time I could feel the passion as Rashad hit me with different strokes. That's when it hit me, this is exactly why I took that charge for his ass! His dick was so fuckin powerful! He's the true definition of what you'd call a dope dick, for real! I closed my eyes tight as I took the pain with his pleasure. His sex was so good it brought tears to my eyes. I even prayed to God that he'd never stop.

"Omg, I'm about to cum!" I whispered as I felt an orgasm coming. Just then, we heard footsteps coming down the stairs. "No! Don't stop, please Rashad!" I begged as I pounded my pussy on the shaft of his big dick.

"I got to!" Rashad whispered as he pulled out and quickly ran to meet Stacey at the stairway.

"What's taking you so damn long!" she said with an attitude as if she suspected something.

"Nothing baby, I was just eating a midnight snack," he explained, as he re-directed her back upstairs.

"Okay, fine Rashad. You just better make some room for this midnight snack too," she said flirtatiously as Rashad followed her back upstairs.

I stood in the darkness, pissed and extremely horny. I needed my husband! I had every mind to bust open their bedroom door and get my husband back. That's exactly what I would've done ten years ago, but now I had a new approach. I wanted Rashad to come back on his own. I wanted him to come back begging on his hands and knees. I wanted him to understand what true love was and to never take it for granted ever again! I slowly pulled my panties back up and walked upstairs to the guest room that was currently my new bedroom. I threw myself on the bed and buried my face into my cold pillow. (*It's going to be a long night*), I cringed, as I tossed and turned before I finally drifted off.

Shortly after, I was awakened by a hand softly covering my mouth. As I opened my eyes, I realized it was Rashad. I quickly remained quiet like he asked.

"You know I always finish what I start," he whispered in my ear as he slowly climbed in bed with me.

I could smell Stacey's cheap perfume all over him. I wanted to tell him to go straight to hell, but who was I fooling? I loved my husband through all his lies and shame. I slowly closed my eyes and gratefully spread my legs. I welcomed every inch of Rashad's manhood as he entered me. He made sure to secure both my wrist so I couldn't leave any evidence of his betrayal. If only he was this careful ten years ago, we wouldn't be in this mess in the first damn place. After we both climaxed, we stared in the each other's eyes. My eyes spoke of passion while Rashad's showed fear.

"Fuck!" he whispered as he finally pulled out of me. "Damn, I fucked up!" he said as he placed his arms over his head.

"What's wrong?" I asked, knowing damn well what was bothering him.

"I just pray you aren't pregnant!" he finally said as he sneaked out my bedroom.

I smiled as I rubbed my belly and held my legs up to give Rashad's sperm a head start. I smiled wickedly as I envisioned the look on Stacey's face when I finally got the chance to tell her I'm pregnant by Rashad. I knew the news would kill her and I didn't care. Rashad was still my husband and she had no business fucking with my man in the first place!

CHAPTER 10

The next morning was just the same as every morning, only difference was me and Rashad shared a secret no one else knew about, except God. I smiled even brighter today and walked with an extra pep to my step.

"Morning Stacey!" I smiled as I approached her downstairs making Rashad breakfast. She looked thunderstruck.

"Morning," she barely mumbled as she looked over at Rashad who sipped his coffee.

"Your grits are burning?" I said as I smiled and looked over at Rashad.

"Shit! My bad, baby," Stacey quickly apologized to Rashad as she poured water over the smoking pan.

"If you want, I can make some more?" She said as she pouted her lips.

"No, it's okay. I'll get something on the road," Rashad said, but his facial expression said something totally different.

"Well, I'm making Junior pancakes and it wouldn't be a problem to make a few more… If that's okay with you Stacey?" I asked as I stared at her for her permission. Stacey eyes looked like they wanted to kill me, but she didn't want to appear insecure in front of Rashad.

"Sure, that's fine Tia. I take mine light and fluffy and so does Rashad," she smiled as if she was saying ha-ha. Little did she know, I already won the game last night and there's a strong possibility of a baby baking out of it.

"No problem, light and fluffy. I got it!" I smiled as I strutted my perfectly plumped ass to the kitchen to make pancakes. Rashad looked at me very suspiciously. He always knew whenever I was up to something, but from the clueless look on his face, he had no idea what I had up my sleeve. After I cooked breakfast, I walked with Junior to his bus stop. He was very quiet this morning.

"Is something wrong, Junior?" I immediately asked. Finally, after a few seconds he responded.

"Are you and dad getting back together?" he asked with a look of excitement in his eyes. I was very shocked by his question and didn't know how to respond.

"I don't know son. Do you think we should get together?" I asked suspiciously as I waited for his opinion.

"Yeah, I guess so," he responded as he shrugged his shoulders, causing me to giggle.

"Well it's settled, we're getting back together," I said with confidence as we finally reached his bus stop.

"But what about Stacey?" he asked with a look of fear on his face. Just then his school bus pulled up.

"Don't worry about Stacey, you just leave her to me," I assured his as I gave him a goodbye hug.

I watched as his bus drove out of sight before I headed home. I quickly searched the internet for jobs in the area.

There were a lot of fast food jobs. I hated fast food and I knew I wasn't the person for that job, especially with my stress. My bad temper mixed with rude customers would only end in disaster. As I scrolled down the list of jobs, I spotted a job position for a cashier at the Publix down the street from my home. I quickly forward my resume and prayed for the best. No one usually wants to hire a convicted felon, especially a murderer. These are the times I wished I never took that charge for Rashad. After sending out my resume to over a hundred jobs, I retired to the kitchen to make a sandwich and catch up on the new TV shows I'd missed in the ten years I'd been gone.

Before I left, I was a diehard fan of *For Your Love*. I was crushed when I discovered it was no longer on air. It had been replaced by *My Wife and Kids* and *The Walking Dead*. After watching TV for a while, my attention was drawn to the front door. I was surprised to see Stacey home so early as she walked through the door. She didn't say anything to me as she quickly walked upstairs. A few seconds later, I heard the shower running. I found that to be very strange. About twenty minutes later, she walked downstairs in a tight blue jeaned dress and some strap up stilettos. It smelled like she poured the whole bottle of cheap perfume on her ass. She quickly grabbed her purse off the table and slammed the door behind her.

I grabbed Rashad's car keys and followed her. I knew Stacey was a certified hoe. She was the type of hoe that didn't have shame. She even fucked her grandmother's husband for his disability check. If you look her up in the dictionary, her name and picture will be under the definition of trifling. My mom always warned me about her, but I had to learn the hard way. Now her trifling ass was laying in my home and sleeping in my marital bed next to my damn husband. Just the thought ran chills down my spine. I was pissed off as I secretly followed her! I couldn't believe my eyes when I followed her to a Comfort Inn Motel.

I carefully parked behind a blue minivan to block Rashad's car. I watched as she stepped out her car and walked in one of the motels' rooms. Shortly after, a man in a brand new 2010 Range Rover parked next to Stacey's Jag and walked in the same motel door. A few seconds later, Stacey opened the door with a smile and escorted the strange man inside. About an hour later, Stacey was leaving the motel. I watched as she quickly got inside her car and drove off. I knew she was heading home to meet Rashad. I decided to take the long route home as I thought long and hard about whether I should tell Rashad. I wanted to tell him the minute I got home, but something told me not to say anything just yet. I guess my curiosity wanted to search for more. I finally pulled up to my home. I noticed Stacey was already inside. I slowly got out the car and walked inside the door. Just as I suspected, she was in the shower. (*Nasty Bitch!*) I thought to myself, as I walked to the kitchen to wash my hands and prepare dinner for Junior and Rashad. Shortly after, Junior and Rashad came through the door.

"Good evening!" I smiled as I took the freshly baked chocolate chip cookies out the oven. Junior's eyes lit up!

"Chocolate chip cookies!" he screamed excitedly as he ran over to grab one.

"I can't lie, it smells very good in here," Rashad complimented.

"Thanks Rashad, there's plenty," I smiled as I held out the pan filled with chocolate chip cookies.

Just then Stacey made her way downstairs in the same red lace night gown I had.

"Hey baby!" she song with excitement as she ran to give Rashad a long, passionate hug.

"Are those baked cookies?" she smiled as she grabbed one of the cookies without asking. "Umm, my favorite!" she winked as she seductively took a bite. I wanted to kill her that very second. Even the look on Rashad's face showed shame.

"Stacey, where is your robe?" he asked as Stacey proudly flaunted her red lace night gown.

"Oh yeah, my bad... We do have company," she smirked as she twisted herself back upstairs.

"Listen Tia, I just want to thank you for all you've been doing around here."

My eyes lit up, because this was the first time in a very long time Rashad had given me a compliment.

"Thanks Rashad," I smiled proudly as I stared in his hazel brown eyes. There was a long awkward pause before Rashad broke the silence.

"Well if you would excuse me, I'm about to take a shower," he said as he walked out the kitchen. I just nodded my head. I knew if he stayed any longer there would be a part two of last night.

After dinner, I played with my son for a while, although my mind was a million miles away. All I could think about was Rashad and how I was dying to tell him about the nasty whore he laid next to every night. After I kissed my son good night, I took a shower and retired to my room. I was so depressed, I didn't want to watch TV. I didn't even go downstairs for my night cup of tea.

Truth is, I didn't want to see Rashad. I couldn't go on pretending that I was okay with him sleeping with another woman, especially the one I once called my sister. My heart was ripping apart and it was all because of him. I felt tears fall down my eyes as the thought of moving on hurt me. I didn't think I could ever move on. I did ten years and the love I had for this man was still the same. Even though he betrayed me in the worst way, my heart still wouldn't allow me to stray. I couldn't believe Stacey could have the only thing I ever wanted, and still want more. She would never love Rashad like I do. Rashad was my first and last man I'd ever touched. He was my soulmate and I loved him to the death of me. They say every woman have that one man they'll sale their soul for.

Unfortunately, that man was Rashad and there's nothing I wouldn't do for him. My thoughts were soon interrupted by a light knock at the door. I quickly wiped my tears as I got up to open the door. Standing at the door was Rashad, holding a cup of tea.

"I see you haven't come down for your tea, and after that great dinner, the least I can do is bring it to you," he smiled, as he handed me the cup of tea.

"Thanks Rashad," I smiled as I slowly closed the door. I quickly took a deep breath, because it was very hard to resist him. But I had to be strong. If he wanted to be with that whore than that's on him. I just prayed he came to his senses very soon.

CHAPTER 11

It'd been three months since I'd been home. I'm very proud of myself, because I've been resisting Rashad's temptation. It has been strictly about my son. It'd also been confirmed that Stacey was cheating. She had been meeting up with the same man about three times a week. I think Rashad suspected something, because he'd been very distant with her lately. She was also pissed with him, because she's ready to get married, but Rashad hasn't approached me anymore about getting a divorce.

Tomorrow is his birthday. Stacey has been running around like a chicken with her head cut off, trying to get the best gift for his special day. She has even let her guard down and asked if I could help cook his surprise dinner. Of course, I said yes. He's the father of my child and still my husband. After a whole day of planning, we were prepared to give him the best Birthday dinner ever! After my bath, I went to the kitchen to get a cup of tea. As expected, Rashad was sitting at the table. It was like he was waiting on me. After I poured a cup of tea, he finally spoke.

"Listen Tia, you know my birthday is tomorrow," he said with a smile on his face.

"Well, actually it's today," I smiled back as I looked at the clock on the wall.

"You right, it is my birthday," he beamed.

"Happy Birthday, Rashad," I cheerfully smiled as I took a seat next to him.

"Thank you, Tia. I can't believe I'm forty," he said as he shook his head in disbelief.

"Me either, old man," I teased, as I admired how fine he still was, even at forty.

"Oh, don't talk, because I do believe someone will be turning thirty-five in a few months," he said with a smirk on his face.

"Please don't remind me!" I cringed at the thought of turning thirty-five.

"So, what are you doing for your birthday?" I quickly asked to change the subject.

"I'm sure Stacey has planned something, but whatever she has planned, I'm not that interested." he said very strangely as stared at me very awkwardly.

"How do you know? You don't even know what she has planned yet," I warned him.

"Unless her plans involve having you, I'm not interested," he said, causing my jaw to drop to the floor.

"What?" I asked, unsure if I heard him correctly.

"You heard me, I want you for my birthday," he finally revealed, causing me to quickly get up from the table to leave.

"Tia, wait!" he called out from the darkness, as he finally stood up.

"Rashad, I don't know what you're doing, but I don't like it at all," I snapped as my frustration became unbearable.

"Just hear me out!" he pleaded as he begged me to come back.

"No, Rashad! If you wanted me, you'd make her leave so we can be a real family again," I demanded.

"Tia, I'm not leaving her. I told you that," he said very seriously, causing my heart to rip from my chest.

"Then we have nothing left to talk about!" I shouted as I stormed upstairs to the guest room.

Shortly after Rashad slowly opened my bedroom door.

"Rashad, please leave!" I cried from all the hurt I felt. Rashad didn't seem to listen as he locked the door behind him and cut off the light.

"What are you doing?" I continued to cry as Rashad made his way in bed with me.

Before I could say anything else, Rashad slowly began kissing me. I tried my hardest to fight him, but Lord knows I'd been missing his touch.

"Why you keep doing this to me?" I cried as he kissed me passionately. He slowly ripped off my night gown as he placed tender kisses all over my body. "Please stop, Rashad!" I begged, but he just ignored me as he continued to kiss me. He quickly pulled my legs apart and didn't waste any time to take a drink from my well.

"Oh God!" I moaned as I felt the warmth of his breath and tongue vigorously licking my special place. It felt so good I was at the point of an orgasm.

"Oh God, right there!" I shouted as I felt myself about to explode! All, of sudden, Rashad stopped. "Please don't stop, I'm about to cum!" I begged as I moved my hips. Just then, Rashad responded.

"Do you love me like you say you love me?" he asked, causing me to open my eyes.

"Of course, I love you, baby," I cried as I tried to push his head back to my special spot.

"I want a threesome," he whispered.

"What did you say?" I asked as my orgasm went out the window.

"You heard me," he said as he put his head back between my legs.

"No, Rashad stop!" I whimpered, as he sped up the motion of his tongue. It became hard for me to think clearly.

"Have a threesome with me, Tia," he said between every lick. I wanted to say no so badly, but the way he was moving his tongue was too good. I was in fear of losing this wonderful feeling. Suddenly, my vagina went numb and the sensation of his tongue brought on the most powerful orgasm I'd ever had.

"I will, I will!" I cried as I orgasmed on his tongue.

After I came, Rashad smirked as he removed his face from between my legs and wiped my juices from his lips. I was now ready for him to bless me up with his dope dick, but he just gently closed my legs.

"You'll get this dick tonight," he promised as he walked out my bedroom. I just laid there staring at the ceiling. (*What the hell have I got myself into now?*), was the only thought in my mind.

CHAPTER 12

I felt the light of day warm my face as it caused me to squint my eyes. I slept terrible! I tossed and turned all night. (*How could I let him trick me like this*), I squirmed as I got out of bed to change my sheets that were stained from the juices of my shame. I quickly walked to the laundry room and dropped my sheets inside the machine. I then headed to the bathroom where I took a long, hot shower. I felt relaxed as the hot water hit my back. I tightly closed my eyes to think of a way to get out of this mess. (*I can't believe he wants me to have a threesome with him and Stacey. The same bitch that ruined our marriage*), I shivered at the thought of it. I became nauseated and felt my vomit making its way to my mouth. I quickly jumped out the shower and hugged the toilet seat as I threw up everything inside me.

"Oh God! I can't believe I let Rashad get me pregnant!" I scold myself as I wiped my vomit from my mouth.

That's another secret I'd been keeping from Rashad. I'm almost three months, but somehow, I'm not showing at all. The only weight I've gained has been to my booty. I think that's the reason Rashad was dying for a threesome with me. I know I'll have to tell him soon, but I don't know how. He has already made it clear that he wasn't leaving Stacey.

After my shower, I managed to pull myself together. I quickly got dressed and hurried downstairs to fix Junior some breakfast. When I made it downstairs, I saw Stacey and Rashad sitting at the kitchen table.

"Where's Junior?" I immediately asked as I looked around the kitchen.

"I let him walk with his friends this morning," Rashad quickly responded.

"But why? You know I always walk with him every morning," I said as I felt hurt by Rashad's decision.

"I know, calm down. It's only for today. Besides, we all need to talk," he smiled, as Stacey held her head down in shame.

"But what about his breakfast, he didn't eat breakfast!" I yelled, as I felt myself begin to panic.

"Tia please! Clam down, I gave him money for breakfast," he assured as he signaled for me join them at the kitchen table. (*I just can't believe he would do that without consulting with me first*), I fumed from inside while I took a seat at the table and folded my arms. After a few seconds of silence, Rashad spoke.

"I just want to thank you ladies for agreeing to make my night special," he gleamed as he looked at the both of us. "Now, I just think we should clear the air before we engage into the fun stuff later tonight," he proudly grinned. "Anyways, I just wanted to confirm that everyone is on board with everything," he said as if we were at a board meeting. I watched as he stared directly at me.

"Rashad, if this is what you really want, I guess I'm fine with it," I said as I forced a smile on my face.

"Thank you, Tia, you are appreciated," he said as he winked over at me. I guess Stacey didn't like his compliment as she rolled her eyes and smacked her lips. "And of course, you are too baby," he smiled as he softly kissed her lips.

"You know I am! I'll do anything, *for my man*!" she said proudly as she winked over at me. Something said just let it go, but it'd be a cold day in hell if I did.

"Well you are definitely right, Stacey. I guess I'm the living proof of what *I'll* do…*for my man*!" I said as I stared back at Rashad who was enjoying the attention.

"I'll see yawl tonight!" I smiled as I grabbed my purse and twisted my big booty to the front door. Before I walked out, I turned around and looked over at Stacey who looked intimidated. "Oh, and by the way… Happy Birthday, baby daddy!" I smiled as I closed the door behind me.

CHAPTER 13

I pulled up at work, I noticed that the parking lot was already crowded. I quickly got out my vehicle and power walked inside. I'd been there for only two months, and I didn't know what they would do without me. When I entered, my manager, Cory, was happy to see me.

"Thank God you're here," he smiled as I walked to clock in.

Cory was a very-handsome black-man in his mid-twenties. He's also in college, working on becoming a pharmacist. He'd been stressing to find someone to fill his position as Manager when he finishes school this year. He's been hounding me to apply for the position, but I refused every time.

"Can you go and relieve Tina?" he asked, looking very stressed.

"Sure!" I smiled as I looked over at the long line of angry customers.

"You think after being here for almost a year, she would know how to work the register by now," he said as he looked over at Tina with a disgusted look on his face.

"Aww, be nice," I warned, as I watched how nervous Tina looked as she fondled with the register.

"I have been. I was supposed to let her go months ago, but I didn't because she's a single parent going through a divorce. I even put her on the express line to make it easier, but look!" he said, as he pointed to Tina and the long line. Somehow, I felt very bad for Tina. I could only imagine what she must be going through. Truth be told, I could be in her shoes any day now.

"Don't fire her, Cory. I'll see to it that she gets it. Just give me a week to work my magic," I pleaded. Cory just smiled and nodded his head.

"Okay, you have one week," he warned as he finally walked off.

When I got to the register, Tina's face was bright red and she was on the verge of crying, because of all the hurtful things the angry customers were saying. I quickly smiled and told her to go on break and I'd take it from here. Tina just nodded her head as she held her head down and walked away. Some of the customers started clapping when I took over. After working for six hours straight, I finally took my break. When I walked inside the break room, Tina was on her phone crying to whom I assumed was her ex-husband.

"Please, just take them for a little while. I don't think I'm going to have a job after today," she cried as she wiped her tears. She didn't even notice I was in the breakroom. "I understand, but can you at least give me some money? I don't have enough for rent and food," she begged, but the bastard was a real asshole.

"All I need is some money for food. Come on, I haven't asked you for a dime in spousal support. The least you can do is help me this one time."

"Hello? Hello!" she shouted as she looked down at her phone. By this time, she realized I was in the break room and put her phone away.

"Is everything alright?" I asked as I took a seat next to her. "Yes, everything is fine," she smiled, but you could obviously see she was hurting bad.

"It's okay, Tina," I whispered as I touched her hand. Tina just stared at me for a minute before she broke down.

"No, it's not okay!" she cried. "He left me for my sister, and has taken everything. I supported that bastard through school. I made sure he had everything! And he still left me... For my sister!" she cried out in the most heartfelt pain. Her situation reminded me of my situation so much.

"It's going to be okay," I assured her. I consoled her as she continued to cry. After about twenty minutes, she finally lifted her head up. Her face was the brighter than red, and her eyes were puffy and full of bags. I could tell she hadn't been getting any sleep.

"Listen, whatever he did, God will punish him. Right now, you must survive for your babies, they need you," I explained as I gave it to her blood raw.

"Cory has been strongly suggesting on firing you, but I told him I will help you. I'll help you get through this. I'm willing to go the extra mile, but I need you to meet me halfway… and if not for you, do it for your kids… they need you and they deserve better than this," I pleaded while Tina took in everything I said. Her face was no longer bright red and she had a look of fight in her eyes.

"I'm ready, Tia. I'm ready to do whatever to get my life back," she said with confidence as she held her head up.

"Good, I'm glad to hear that. Now we just need to get the cash register down, and you will be ready to take over the world," I said as we both laughed.

*****

Later that day, Cory allowed me and Tina to take the last hour so I could teach her how to work the register properly. After twenty minutes, Tina had finally gotten the hang of it.

"See, I knew you could do it!" I smiled as I hugged her.

"Wow. Thanks, Tia. Thanks for believing in me," she thanked me as she almost suffocated me by the tightness of her chubby arms.

"You're welcome," I smiled as I looked down at my watch. I couldn't believe it was time for to go.

"See you tomorrow," Tina smiled as I waved her off.

I slowly walked to clock out. Usually I'm so happy to get home to see my son, but today I wished I could've worked all night. As I made it to my car, I popped in my Alicia Keys Cd, and sung to the words of *Unthinkable*. I had a strong liking for that song. As I made it to my home, I parked in the driveway next to Rashad and Stacey's car. I slowly took a breath, cut the car off, and walked inside. The house was very quiet.

"Where's Junior?" I asked as I saw Stacey and Rashad sitting on the couch.

"He's at my mom's house," he smiled as he signaled me to the living room.

"Yes, Rashad!" I responded, as I rolled my eyes.

"I want to start soon as possible," he said impatiently like a little kid in a candy store.

"Baby, be patient!" Stacey giggled as she rubbed Rashad's head. "I'm preparing you a delicious dinner," she smiled as she licked her lips seductively.

(*I can't believe this bitch is taking credit for the dinner I cooked*), I cringed, as I gave Stacey a mean look.

"Oh, and with the help of Tia," she smirked, as she rolled her eyes.

"Well thank you ladies, I'm certain dinner will be perfect," he smiled graciously as he grabbed the front of his pants.

"Bae, go upstairs!" Stacey yelled as she pulled Rashad from the couch. "I'll be up in a minute to run your bath water," she smiled as she flirtatiously rubbed the front of his pants.

"Okay, hurry up!" Rashad warned as he slowly walked upstairs.

After Rashad made it upstairs, Stacey quickly turned to me. "Okay, now that Rashad is gone… I think it's time that we talk, woman to woman," she said as she took a seat at the kitchen table and crossed her bony legs. "Now, just so you know… this is a one-time thing," she said as she stared at me with a look of disgust.

"Oh, trust me, I already know!" I quickly responded while giving her an equal look of disgust.

"Okay, because I don't want you to get the wrong idea that Rashad still wants you," she warned as she looked me up and down.

"Oh, I could never get the wrong idea, especially if it's written so perfectly," I smiled, as I poured myself a small glass of red wine.

"Oh, and what idea would that be?" she responded while looking unpoised. I quickly took a small sip from my wine glass and smiled.

"Come on Stacey, you're smarter than that. Out of all the women in Tampa, he's dying to have a threesome with little-ole me? Don't you think that's odd?" I said sarcastically as I slowly twisted over to the kitchen table to join her.

"Bitch, please!" she grinned while shaking her head as if she was un-bothered, but the look up her face showed insecurity.

"It's okay to be scared, not everyone was born with this gift," I assured her.

"And what gift might that be?" she asked as she sucked her teeth.

"Oh, you'll soon see," I said with confidence as I left the kitchen table, leaving Stacey to sweat.

CHAPTER 14

After Rashad's birthday dinner and hearing Stacey's lying ass take credit for my cooking, I finally submerged my body inside the hot bubble bath I'd filled with lavender oil to calm myself. In the next hour, I would be engaging in a threesome with Rashad and my worst enemy. I slowly closed my eyes as I tried to meditate. I kept telling myself it would be fine and I was only doing this to get my family back. I also convinced myself that I was just acting out a role. This had nothing to do with my beliefs, and I'm definitely not a lesbian. I closed my eyes as I sank my body deeper into the hot bath.

After about forty minutes, I final got out the tub. I knew it wouldn't be long before Stacey and I would be fulfilling Rashad's dirty birthday wish. I shook my shoulders like a baseball player would do before every game. Deep inside, this was a game for me. A game between me and Stacey, and the prize was Rashad. (*I just had to have him!*) I desperately thought, as I looked for the sexiest lingerie I owned.

I came across the lingerie I wore my wedding night and smiled. I remembered how I rocked Rashad's world in that very same lingerie. I just had to wear it tonight, because I knew it was very special to the both of us. I smiled to see that it still fit, but even better this time. I looked very naughty in my black leather. I quickly slipped on my matching black leather thigh high boots. I smiled confidently as I strutted downstairs to the living room. When I made it to the bottom of the stairs, Stacey and Rashad's mouths dropped. Stacey looked like an ant compared to the sun. I was shining! Rashad knew he couldn't say anything, or Stacey would have killed him. She looked intimidated as she wore the ugliest lime green lingerie I'd ever seen. I slowly twisted myself inside the living room. I made sure to stand directly in front of Rashad, while Stacey held her head down.

"Do you ladies want a drink?" he smiled as he looked me up and down.

"Yes, I'll love a drink," I said while I gave Rashad my best smile as I sat next to Stacey on the leather couch and crossed my smooth caramel legs.

Shortly after, Rashad came back with three wine glasses. Stacey was so stressed, she quickly gulped down her glass of wine.

"Alright baby, don't get too drunk," Rashad warned her.

"Oh baby, being drunk is a good thing. You know how I perform when I'm drunk," she said as she gave Rashad a flirtatious wink.

"In that case, here's some more," Rashad smiled as he poured Stacey another glass.

"Damn Stacey, that's just too bad," I said as I shook my head in shame.

"And why is that?" She said as she folded her arms.

"No reason, I guess some people are naturally freaky. You see, I never needed wine to get me in the mood," I smiled as I took a very small sip before I put down my wine glass.

Rashad immediately started laughing as he passionately stared at me.

"Oh, I'm freaky!" Stacey said as she looked over at Rashad who was enjoying the debate.

"Well show me how freaky you can get?" Rashad said, putting Stacey on the spot.

That was all he had to say before Stacey stood up and walked over to Rashad. She didn't waste any time, as she slowly stripped out of her bright green lingerie. I couldn't believe how many stretch marks Stacey had, because the bitch had never been pregnant a day of her life. Her breasts even sagged, which was crazy being that she wore an A cup. (*This is what Rashad left me for?*) I thought as I began to smirk.

I watched as Stacey pulled Rashad's boxers to his ankles and pushed him on the couch. She quickly got on her knees and tried to take Rashad in her mouth. I can't even lie, I was excited to see this, because Rashad's dick was so huge, I even had a hard time putting it inside my mouth. But after years of practice, I got it all in like a pro. I watched as she put just the head in her mouth. She sucked Rashad's dick with no excitement. She even used her hands to block his manhood for going deep inside her mouth. This bitch sucked terribly at sucking dick. I smiled as I watched her performance, because she didn't have shit on me.

After a few minutes in, Rashad quickly called me over. The look on his face showed boredom. I watched as Stacey slowly got off her knees and rolled her eyes. I was now up to bat, and I was confident I would knock it out the park.

"Get your ass up, Rashad!" I demanded, as I waited for him to do as I said. Immediately, Rashad was on his feet. He stood at six-foot-two. He was a giant next to me, but I was nowhere near intimated.

"I'm going to suck you dry!" I said while I stared into his hazel brown eyes. That was the last thing I said to him before I was on my knees with all his dick inside my mouth.

"Shit!" Rashad moaned, as I bobbed my head up and down on his manhood.

Stacey stood in silence with her mouth opened in shock. Just hearing Rashad moan made me moan, too. I loved pleasing him, and making him cum made me orgasm. I wasn't down there for two minutes, before Rashad had oozed everywhere. I smiled as Rashad's cum rained with victory. I won before it had even started. Rashad had cum so hard, he was literally drained. His poor manhood tried it's best to recover, but it was no use. Stacey was so pissed that she stormed upstairs and slammed their bedroom door. Rashad didn't even care, because he'd had the best head of his life.

He just smiled before he finally said, "thank you."

"No problem Rashad," I smiled as I walked upstairs to wash away his semen.

After my shower, I laid on my bed with a smile on my face. I was happy how things had turned out, but I was even happier that I didn't have to touch Stacey's ass. I had satisfied Rashad, without the help of Stacey. I finally yawned as I closed my eyes. I knew tomorrow would be a good day.

CHAPTER 15

The next day, I headed to the bathroom to brush my teeth and prepare for a great day. After I brushed my teeth, I quickly walked downstairs. I wanted to make Rashad breakfast before he went to work. They say a happy woman will cook just about everything for the right man! I guess that's true, because I happily made Rashad just about everything I knew he liked. I cooked bacon, eggs, grits and French toast. I even made my mother's homemade biscuits he always loved. I heard footsteps making their way down the stairs. I just knew it was Rashad. Like I predicted, it was Rashad, with Stacey right behind him.

"Good morning, Rashad!" I said with a prideful smile on my face. Rashad just looked at me for a brief second and walked out the door without saying a word. I couldn't believe it! It was like he was a different person. It was like he became Satan overnight. I felt my heart shatter as I looked at all the food I had prepared for him.

All, of sudden, Stacey started laughing.

"Rashad and I want to thank you for last night," she smirked as she put a strip of bacon inside her mouth. "But Rashad has told me to let you know that your service is no longer needed and your divorce papers are on your bed waiting to be signed," she smiled as she walked out the door.

I felt my heart drop out my chest. I felt played out like an old book of food stamps. I quickly threw off my cooking robe and ran upstairs. My heart sank to my stomach as I walked inside my bedroom door. On my bed, just as Stacey had said, were the divorce papers, a pen and forty dollars. I couldn't believe my eyes! To add insult to injury, he'd left behind forty dollars like I was some junkie ass prostitute who had sucked his dick for a quick fix. I was so distraught as I picked up the divorce papers. I honestly didn't know how much more I could take.

"Maybe I should sign the damn divorce papers and get on with my life, but how? My whole life revolves around Rashad. If I can't be with him, I might as well roll over and die!"

The thought of living without Rashad had broken my heart. I don't know why, especially after the many times he ripped my heart out of my chest.

"There's just no way I could ever sign this!" I mumbled to myself, as I grabbed the papers and ripped them in tiny pieces along with the forty dollars and threw it by their bedroom door.

I quickly rush downstairs to get Rashad's car keys from its usual spot, but they were gone. I immediately ran outside to see Rashad had taken his car. I had been so badly hurt by Rashad that I couldn't shed anymore tears, even if I tried. I took a deep breath and walked to the bus stop. I felt like a zombie as I slowly walked down the street. It was like I was here physically, but mentally I had checked out.

After waiting at the bus stop for almost thirty-minutes, the city bus had finally come. After a long miserable ride, I finally made it to work. For the first-time ever, I was late for work. I immediately ran to clock-in. Before I could turn around, Cory was standing right behind me.

"I never thought I'd see the day you're late," Cory smiled as he looked at his watch.

"I'm sorry Cory, but my car has broken down this morning," I lied, while Cory looked at me strangely.

"Damn, how does a brand new 2010 Jag breaks down?" he curiously asked with a smirk on his face. I could tell he wasn't buying my story.

"Yeah, I'm surprised too," I smiled as I quickly walked away before he could ask any more questions.

*****

After a long work day, I finally clocked out. I tried to avoid Corey and my coworkers, because I immediately had a bus to catch. Just as I was walking out the door, Cory stopped me.

"Tia!" he shouted, as he waved for me to come back. (*Damn!*) I said to myself as I slowly turned back around. "How did you get to work this morning?" he said while looking suspiciously.

"I caught the city bus," I lightly mumbled as I held my head down in shame.

"The city bus?" Cory said as if that was some sort of joke to him.

"Yes, and if you can excuse me, I have a bus to catch," I said as I slowly turned back around.

"I'm not about to let you catch a bus, Tia," he said as he shook his head.

"I remember all the crazy folks I used to encounter when I used to catch the bus... and I'm a man, so I can only imagine the crazy people you'll have to deal with," he laughed, causing me to smirk a bit.

"I'll take you home," he demanded, and from the look on his face, it wasn't negotiable.

I wanted to refuse, because I didn't want Rashad to get the wrong impression. But, on the other hand, maybe if Rashad see me with another man it would open his eyes.

"Sure, I would love that," I smiled as I watched Cory's eyes light up. Without anything else to say, we headed to his black Mercedes. He quickly opened the door for me as I got in. (*Damn, I never had Rashad to open the car door for me*), I thought to myself. As we rode home, I couldn't help but to feel the awkwardness coming from the unusual silence. This had made me feeling very uncomfortable.

"So, when will you be done with school?" I asked to get rid of the awkwardness.

"I'll be officially done next month," he smiled proudly.

"Well, congratulations," I smiled, as I thought about how great he must be feeling. I began to think about how great I felt when I received my RN license. That was one the happiest days of my life, because I'd worked so hard to get it.

I soon felt sadness as I thought about how quickly I'd lost everything.

"So how long have you been married?" Cory asked as he glimpsed at my wedding ring.

"For twelve years now," I said proudly as I admired my three-carat diamond ring.

It had hit me that my thirteen-year anniversary was around the corner, Christmas day to be exact.

Christmas of 94 was the best day of my life. That was the day Rashad had proposed to me. He put my engagement ring inside a Christmas stocking. I thought, and still think, that was the best engagement ever.

"Well, he sure is a lucky man!" Cory responded, causing me to snap out of the world I had been daydreaming in.

"Thank you, Cory. That's very nice of you," I smiled as I enjoyed the compliment. Although, Rashad couldn't see it, I was happy another man did. Shortly after, we pulled up to my house.

As I was getting out the car and thanking Cory for the ride home, Rashad had pulled inside the driveway. Cory looked shocked to see my car wasn't broken down. Before things could get any worse, I quickly tried to wave him off, but Cory didn't move. His face showed the look of shock mixed with confusion as he soon witnessed my husband greeting another woman with a long, passionate kiss.

I was so embarrassed that I quickly walked inside my house and refused to look back. I was so humiliated and on the verge of tears, as I bypassed my son and ran upstairs to my room. I couldn't believe Cory had to witness my shocking secret. I was so distraught by what just happened that I laid in my bed and cried for hours.

(There's no way in hell, I could ever show my face at work ever again!) I thought to myself as I cried my eyes out.

After bawling my eyes out for hours, I finally pulled myself together and walked to my son's bedroom. He was so busy playing his new video game he didn't notice I was standing behind him.

"Can I play?" I asked as I waited for him to respond.

"Hey mom, I didn't know you were there," he smiled, as I sat down next to him. He didn't waste any time passing me a controller.

We sat in silence as we played his Xbox. After twenty minutes, I finally broke the silence.

"So, how would you feel if I was to get my own place?" I asked nervously as I waited for his response.

"Why are you moving? You don't like it here?" Junior asked as his interest for the game soon died. He was staring at me with full attention.

"Yes, I love it here, but I think it's for the best that I move," I tried my best to explain without breaking down into tears.

"Is it something I did?" Junior mumbled, causing my heart to fall to the floor.

"Of course, not!" I said firmly as I looked him deep into his hazel brown eyes.

"Then why are you moving?" he asked, as he held his head down.

"Your father and I have outgrown each other and it's time I had my own place for a little while," I explained as I prepared myself for more questions.

"Can I come live with you?" he quickly asked, but this time he made sure his eyes were staring clear into mine.

"Yes, I would love for you to live with me, but right now… you need to stay with your father, but only for a little while," I assured him.

"How long?" he pouted as he folded his tiny arms and gave me the cutest puppy dog eyes.

"Not long, baby boy," I smiled, as I wrapped my arm around him to console him… "Very soon it'll be just me, you and your father, and were going to live happily ever after!" I promised.

"But what about Stacey?" he mumbled as he rolled his eyes as if I was lying.

"Don't you worry about Stacey, I'll handle that," I promised. "But, in the meantime, the only thing you need to worry about is this butt kicking I'm about to give you!" I smiled as I grabbed the controller. Junior smiled, as he quickly picked his controller back up.

"Over my dead body, mom!" he said wickedly as he pressed very hard on his controller.

I'll Always Be Down for My Man

After playing multiple games on Junior's Xbox, we finally called it a night as I tucked him in, and kissed his forehead.

"I love you mom," Junior whispered, causing my heart to melt.

"I love you even more!" I finally responded, before I walked out his bedroom door.

I quickly headed downstairs to the kitchen. I couldn't believe Stacey had cooked hotdogs for dinner again! I looked at the leftover hotdogs with disgust and quickly moved them to the side.

It was very clear that Stacey didn't give a damn about Rashad or what he ate. When I was with Rashad, he had full course meals every night. It's just too bad he would trade home cooked meals for hotdogs. I quickly pulled the luncheon meat out the refrigerator and made a quick sandwich and some tea.

As I was eating, I heard footsteps coming down the stairs. I prayed it was Rashad, but I was wrong. I watched as Stacey walked in the kitchen, wearing Rashad's old basketball jersey. The same one I would always wear. I knew Stacey was only trying to start some shit, because she knew how much I loved to wear that jersey. (*I just can't believe this bitch has the nerves to flaunt it in front of me*), My thoughts escaped. I stared at her like she'd lost her damn mind.

"Well, hello Tia," she smirked as she pulled the strawberries from out the refrigerator.

I just stood in silence as I continued to eat my turkey sandwich. I prayed she wouldn't say anything else to me, or I would hurt her badly. But this time Rashad wouldn't be able to save her.

"Rashad loves him some strawberries," she smiled as she grabbed the whip cream too.

I could feel my anger broiling, as I tried my best to remain calm.

"Anyways, have a good night…Oh, and try to stay warm," she winked as she pointed at Rashad's jersey.

That remark was the feather that broke the camel's back. Suddenly, I was seeing in red as I entered the gates of hell. I quickly jumped up from the table and grabbed the back of Rashad's jersey. I yanked the jersey so hard, Stacey's skinny ass flew back.

"Rashad!" she screamed, as I continued to tug at the jersey.

She tried her best to hold onto the jersey, but I was determined that jersey was coming off her dirty ass body.

"Rashad, come quick!" she screamed as she covered her face.

Little did she know, I wasn't interested in laying a finger on her. I just wanted that jersey off her ass, as I pulled on it for dear life. I pulled so hard, I ripped Rashad's jersey in shreds. There she stood naked on the kitchen floor as she tried her best to cover her body with the shreds from his jersey. Just then Rashad came running downstairs. He looked shocked to see Stacey laying on the floor naked and his jersey ripped to shreds.

"Tia! What the fuck have you done?" he asked in disbelief.

"What the hell have you done?!" I screamed, as I thought about how disrespectful he was to allow Stacey to wear that particular jersey.

"How could you let her wear that, Rashad?" I asked, as I felt very hurt and betrayed, because that was the jersey he wore when he had taken my virginity.

"That jersey holds many memories for me, and you will be that damn stupid to allow her to wear it, huh?" I shouted as I felt myself beginning to get even more angry.

"First off, you need to calm the fuck down!" he warned as looked at me like I had lost my damn mind.

"Second, that isn't your jersey, it's mine! Third, I can let whoever I want wear it. And lastly, what gives you the right to destroy my fuckin' property?" he asked while looking very pissed.

"You know what Rashad… Fuck you!" I screamed very intensely as I ran back upstairs.

I couldn't believe Rashad didn't show any sympathy for me. That was it, I had to leave this hell that was once a home for me. I quickly packed my bags, because soon as morning hit, I was out of here. I wrote Rashad a letter, something I'd been doing for the ten years I been locked down. The only difference was this letter was different from any letter I'd written before. This wasn't a love letter, but more of a promise letter.

The letter read:

To my husband,

I have loved you for many years. Even with all the love I given you, you only repaid me with tears. I love you to the point that I'm crazy. I am crazy for the sacrifices I've made for your selfish love. Am I sorry? That's a question that I hate to answer, because truth is... I'm not! Even with all of me, somehow you still wanted more. I can't lie, "the more" that you requested, I've cried many nights to have her place. Just to be near you and share your space is all I ever needed. Somehow, what I needed, has gotten me mistreated and brought me to pure shame. The worst pain I ever felt was from your name. Rashad. A name that brings flames to my special place and a hurricane to my heart. How could that be? Am I the same me? How could she be better than me? Are the question that remains a mystery. I'm just praying one day these questions will be removed and all my insecurities will be replaced with kisses and of you holding me. Somehow, I still believe that will one day be, but until that day. I will respect your wishes and leave. Until next time my one true love.

Ps. I'm leaving you with your peace and temporary happiness, because one day I'll be back. This is just something I got to do For My Man.

Love, Tia!

CHAPTER 16

Before morning could shine brightly through the window blinds, I got up and snuck down the hall to my son's bedroom. He was still sleeping when I made my way inside. I placed the letter I'd written him next to his pillow and gently kissed his cheek. I then quietly walked downstairs with my suitcase in hand and waited for the cab to take me to the nearest motel. Shortly after, the cab pulled inside the driveway. I quickly opened the door before he could blow his horn and wake everyone. I slipped the letter into Rashad's slightly cracked window, and I was off. After driving around for almost an hour, I finally found a decent motel. I gave my cab driver sixty dollars and exited the cab. I paid my room up for about three weeks, because that was all the time I needed to get my family back. I had a plan. I was going to expose Stacey for the low-down, dirty whore she has always been. *Once I provide Rashad with quality evidence, he will then see Stacey for who she is,* I thought to myself as I laid down on the small motel bed. I closed my eyes, because I knew tomorrow would start the first day of my operation I called "For My Man." I know I needed plenty sleep so I could have a clear head tomorrow. Without any more stress, I peacefully closed my eyes and tried my best to shut out any thoughts of Rashad. I was somehow very confident that operation, For My Man, would be successful. It wasn't long before I was in a deep sleep.

*****

The next morning, I was up bright and early. I called the same cab driver from yesterday. He personally gave me his number, so whenever I needed a ride, I could call him directly. Just as he promised, he was outside my motel room within five-minutes. I quickly combed my hair, pulled it inside a secure ponytail, and grabbed my purse as I walked out the door. The driver smiled hard when he saw me. He appeared to be of a Haitian descent. He had a very strong accent, and looked to be in his late forties. I could tell from his cheesy grin he possibly wanted more, but it's too bad, because he would never get it from me. The only thing I was prepared to do was bless him with my charming smile to get my fare lowered, or possibly free rides.

"Where to, beautiful," he smiled flirtatiously, exposing his single gold tooth.

"To the Publix a few blocks up," I smiled as I bat my pretty brown eyes at him.

"Okay, no problem dear," he winked as he finally pulled out of the motel's parking lot.

Shortly after, we pulled inside of Publix's parking lot. I quickly glanced at the meter and handed him eight-dollars. "Oh no, this one is free," he refused while winking his rheumy eyes, causing me to almost gag.

"Thank you," I fraudulently smiled as I exited his vehicle.

"Don't forget to call me whenever you need me beautiful," he shouted, making sure I heard him. But I didn't bother to look back. I swiftly walked inside the store and headed-straight to the back to clock in. I prayed I wouldn't bump into Cory. (*Well, so much for prayers*), I thought to myself as I saw him walk up.

"Hey Tia, how's it going?" he asked, with a strong look of concern.

"I'm fine! Why?" I snapped, as I didn't have time for his beating around the bush questions.

"If there's something you like to ask me, then get it off your chest, for Christ sake!" I said very snubbed, while Cory looked as if I had clearly check out.

"Calm down Tia, I only asked how you been. I didn't mean to offend you," he quickly apologized.

"I'm sorry, Cory. I guess I'm having a bad day, is all," I shamefully apologized. I knew Cory didn't mean any harm, I guess I was still paranoid.

"Listen Tia, I'm not trying to be in your business, but I just want you to know that you deserve better. Any man would love to have you. I for damn sure would!"

Before I could address what he just said, or defend my fucked-up marriage by explaining Rashad's neurotic behavior, Cory was already gone. I guess he refused to stand around while I fed him garbage.

*****

After a long work day, I finally clocked out and called my personal cab driver. Like before, he was here within five-minutes. I got in the cab and requested that he take me to the used car dealership down the street from my job.

"Why do you need to go there?" He asked with a dim look on his face.

"Because I need a car," I responded as I rolled my eyes at his dumb-ass question.

He didn't say anymore as we rode in silence. We soon pulled inside the used car lot. I quickly stepped out and told him he didn't have to wait on me. He immediately rolled his eyes as he demanded twelve-dollars.

"Excuse me, I only owe you four-dollars," I said as I looked at the meter.

"You owe me eight-dollars from this morning," he reminded me with his hand held-out.

(I couldn't believe this man) as I dug in my purse and threw him twenty-dollars.

"Keep the change!" I said with utter disgust as I forcefully slammed the door and walked inside the car dealership.

I couldn't understand how crazy some men could be. It was hell dealing with Rashad's demented-ass, but to entertain another man's foolishness was too much for me to entertain. I'm just grateful I will no longer have to deal with him ever again after today. I had saved up five-thousand dollars, and I was ready to buy the 2006 Chevy Impala that captured my attention. I was fortunate to see it was still available.

I immediately told the salesman what car I was interested in. He smiled like he saw dollar signs, and made sure to brag on every detail about the car.

After talking until he was blood red in the face, I finally accepted. I could tell from his face he wanted to jump up and down, but he maintained his cool salesman attitude. After all the paperwork, I was finally handed the keys to my brand-new car, although, it was four-years old. I proudly put the key in the ignition and drove off. I immediately drove to the Comfort-Inn, I knew Stacey would soon be at.

As I expected, Stacey's white Jag was pulled next to the same 2010 Range Rover. I quickly got out my car and walked upstairs. I waited by their room door with my phone. I was ready to record her the minute she stepped foot out the door. I also put my ear to the door so I could listen. I could hear a lot of arguing coming from inside. I pushed my ear even closer to the door to make out what they were talking about.

"Fuck that! I'm ready to do that nigga today!" the male's voice demanded.

"I know, but you got to wait. I need him to marry me first, so I can reap from his policy," Stacey shockingly replied. I couldn't believe what I was hearing, as I held my stomach.

"You supposed to have been married that nigga!" the unknown man impatiently shouted.

"I know, but that bitch won't sign the divorce papers," Stacey explained, causing cold chills to run down my spine.

"Man, do what you got to do! If she won't sign the divorce papers, kill her ass!" he strongly advised her, causing me to shake like a dope fiend in rehab.

"Either way, that pussy is still a dead man, I promise!" he shouted as he hit the wall with his fist, I assumed. I couldn't stand to hear anymore. I was petrified as I swiftly ran downstairs to my car.

My head was spinning as I tried to catch my breath. I thought I'd pass out any minute. I quickly cut on my air conditioner to cool myself. I knew Stacey was up to no good. She had been plotting on Rashad all this time, but why? Why does that guy want Rashad dead? That was the million-dollar question that needed to be answered the most. It's just too bad I didn't have a clue to the reason why.

I staked out in the parking lot waiting for them to come out. About an hour later, I spotted Stacey coming out the motel room. The way she looked around showed her guilt as she quickly hopped in her car and sped off. I just couldn't believe that Stacey had been setting Rashad up all this time. I honestly believed her interest in Rashad was personal, but damn was I wrong.

A few seconds later, this Big Suge Knight looking brother with tattoos in his face walked out the motel room. I quickly adjusted my seat so he couldn't see me. I waited until he backed out the parking lot before I started following him. I followed him on the interstate going South. I was surprised when I realized the guy didn't live in Tampa. We had entered the city of Saint Petersburg.

We ended up at some house with a yard full of people. I quickly cut my lights off as I watched him stepped out his car. I watched as he chatted with some of the people outside before he walked inside this unknown house. I realized he must live at that location, because he never came back out, at least for the time I spent spying. I slowly drove off and headed back to Tampa. I didn't know what I was about to get myself into, but I knew I had to be careful. I also knew it wouldn't be long before Stacey took that man's advice, because I wasn't signing any papers. Rashad and I are in this to death do us part, whether he likes it or not.

I finally made it back to Tampa. I pulled into the driveway of the home I'd just moved out of. I didn't waste any time as I heavily knocked on the door. A few seconds later, Stacey opened the door.

"Hey Stacey, I'm here to visit my son," I said as politely as possible.

"Okay, come on in," she smiled, as if she was the most innocent woman in the world, but deep inside she was Satan in a dress.

"Junior! Your mom is here!" she yelled from downstairs. Shortly after, all you could hear was loud footsteps as Junior ran downstairs and wrapped his arms around me.

"Mom, I missed you!" he said with so much exhilaration.

"I missed you too," I smiled, as I appreciated the hug we shared. "Let's go play," I whispered inside his ears as Stacey watched from the kitchen.

"Okay, yawl have fifteen-minutes, then it's time for his dinner," she warned.

I found that to be very strange. (*Stacey never cooked before, but now she's cooking today?*) I thought to myself, as I gave her a suspicious look and slowly walked upstairs to play with my son.

After playing with my son for almost an hour, Stacey finally called upstairs for Junior to eat. (*I'd be damn if she tries to poison my son.*)

"Junior, I was thinking we should go to Mc Donald's," I said with a smile on my face. That was all I had to say before Junior's face lit up.

"Yes!" Junior cheered as he quickly grabbed his Nikes and put them on his feet. As we walked downstairs, we were greeted by Stacey.

"Go wash your hands so you can eat," she demanded while she poured slop inside his plate.

"That's okay Stacey, I'm taking him to Mc Donald's," I smiled as I looked at how happy Junior was to not be eating the dog shit Stacey prepared.

"I don't think that's a good idea," she immediately interrupted as she looked very strangely at me.

"It's not what you think, I'm his mother, remember?" I quickly responded as Junior and I bypassed her and walked out the door.

Once we got in my car, I warned Junior not to eat anything in that house unless I tell him it's okay.

He didn't understand why, but he still nodded his head and looked out the window.

"I will be over to feed you every day from now on, okay?" I assured him as I waited on him to respond.

"Are you going to take me to Mc Donald's every day?" he smiled brightly, showing of his beautiful deep dimples.

"We will see, Junior," I smiled, as I pulled up to Mc Donald's. After we ate, we drove around and talked for a while. I was surprised when he revealed that his father had been sick for almost three-weeks. I knew something was extremely wrong. I never known Rashad to ever be sick, not even once! I also told him I had a special gift for him. He immediately became cheerful as he begged to know what is was, but I told him in six months he will know. I watched as Junior folded his arms.

"That's too long, I want it know," he pouted. (*He is so adorable!*), I thought to myself, as I drove him back home. When we made it back in, I saw Stacey walking to the laundry room with a blanket with some weird stains on it.

"Where's my daddy?" Junior asked with a look of concern on his face.

"He's upstairs, lying down. He doesn't seem to be feeling well. I think he has the flu or something?" she explained as she held her head down, which showed an ultimate-sign of guilt.

"Hmm, that's very strange," I said as I looked at the stains on the blanket.

"What's strange?" Stacey defensively barked as she quickly threw the puke filled blanket inside the machine.

"Nothing, it's just that Rashad has never been sick before. Even as a little boy, he has never had a cold," I said as I watched her suspiciously.

"Well, it's the first time for everything," she huffed as she stormed back upstairs.

I waited until she closed their bedroom door before Junior and I walked upstairs. I quickly tucked him in and warned him not to unlock his bedroom door for anyone, unless it's me or his father.

"Okay mom," he whispered as he slowly closed his eyes and drifted off to sleep.

On my way home, I thought long and hard on how I was going to stop Stacey. I knew I could never tell Rashad, because he would swear I'm just jealous of their relationship. I needed stronger evidence and I was determined to get it! Before I went home, I decided to visit my mother's grave-site. I hadn't been to her grave since we buried her. I just couldn't stomach the fact that my mother wasn't no longer here. I always thought she'd be here. Even when mom was on her death bed, I always thought she'd survive her battle with AIDS. Tonight, I have realized just how alone I really was. As I looked at her tombstone, tear streamed from my eyes.

"Mama, I need you!" I cried-out as I tightly hugged her tombstone. "I don't know what to do! I'm falling apart. My family has been destroyed! I don't know what to do, or where to turn. I miss you mommy!" I wept as the desperation of wanting my mother tore at my heart. I laid on her grave as if she'd come from her casket and give me the answers to all my problems. I knew I was on the verge of crazy. I slowly wiped my bloodshot eyes and quietly walked back to my car, and headed to the motel I been living at. I took a long bath and read my bible before I finally drifted-off to sleep.

CHAPTER 17

After two-weeks of following Stacey around, I learned that
Stacey was being paid to set up Rashad. I watched on multiple
occasions, the strange man handing her stacks of money, and
she would leave shortly after. For what? I still don't know.
All I do know was Rashad had been constantly sick with flu
like symptoms. I been very worried about him lately.

After I clocked out, I went directly to the pharmacy
department to buy Rashad some Flu medicine. It's not
certain that Stacey was the reason for Rashad's sickness, but I
wouldn't be a surprise if she was. As I paid for the medicine
and was about to leave, I heard a man's voice yell my name.

"Tia King!" a white man in a very expensive Armani suit
shouted.

"Yes?" I said as I waited to hear what business this man
could possibly have with me.

"Are you Tia King?" he asked once more, as if he was
making sure he had the right person.

"Yes, I'm Tia King… Why?" I asked unaware of how he
knew my name.

"Tia King, you have been served, good day," he smirked as
he handed me some papers out of his briefcase.

I couldn't believe my eyes as I read the papers. The letter
stated that I had been subpoenaed to court for a divorce

hearing. I immediately began to panic as I ran out the store. Reality had hit me like a ton of hard bricks. I could feel my whole life drifting away.

Rashad couldn't divorce me yet. I was pregnant with his child. He would also be letting go of his one true love. I refused to let our love die! I had to tell Rashad what was going on, I just prayed that he believed me.

CHAPTER 18

Divorce Court

I couldn't believe I would see the day Rashad and I would be standing in a courtroom in front of the judge for a divorce. Rashad and I had been through so much together. We held many dark secrets that we vowed to take to our graves. From the outside looking in, we were the picture-perfect couple. We had always been far from that. I guess that's what made us the perfect match. You see, we both had a mysterious side, which was very rare to most. We were, without a doubt, the modern-day Bonnie and Clyde. We had each other's back through the good times and bad. I was so in love with Rashad, and there was nothing I wouldn't do for him.

I was even there for him when his mother and father were murdered in their home a month before our wedding. Rashad never shed a tear when he got the news. It wasn't that he didn't love his parents or anything like that. Rashad was born without emotions. That was only because, as a little boy, his parents had already prepared him for the worst. They were heavily in the dope game. His parents had central and south Florida on lock. I guess they always knew someone would off them one day. That was the risk that came with the game. Their only request was for Rashad to make a promise that if anything happened to them, he would avenge their deaths and take over the family business. Rashad did just that!

His only focus at that time was to seek revenge and live the life that was inherited to him. He didn't waste any time putting the word in the streets. He already knew the streets lived by the no snitch code, but he also knew ten-stacks will make the most loyal come forward. As you know, crackheads are the first to come forward, especially when money was involved. So, it wasn't a surprise when crackhead Larry came through with the news. After he told Rashad who killed his parents, Rashad paid him as promised, but before he could make it out the abandoned building, Rashad had called him back. He soon gave me the eye and I knew exactly what time it was. Rashad handed me his Beretta to smoke the crackhead while he had later set fire to the man that killed his parents. Rashad said it was a task to prove my loyalty to him and to honor his deceased parents. As much as my mind told me no, my heart said pull the trigger. Without any further regrets, I followed my heart. I took a deep breath, closed my eyes and squeezed the trigger. We didn't even stick around to watch his body drop. When I looked-over at Rashad, he was smiling very proudly.

"No witnesses, no crimes!" he stated with a smile on his face as we swerved through traffic.

Later that night, we made the most-passionate love ever! We also vowed to take that night to our graves. That was also the night we decided to start our family.

Now can you see why I'm fighting for my marriage? I've done so much to prove my love to Rashad. I even sold my soul to the devil for his ass. Now, as I stand in this cold as courtroom to defend my love, I also stand here confused. Our love for each other used to run blood deep, but now it's as shallow as a puddle. Hell, there was time when Rashad wouldn't even take God's word over mine. Now he trusted Stacey's scandalous-ass over me. That night after I received my subpoena, I went to his house to warn him about Stacey, but he refused to speak to me. He even went as far as banning me from coming to see our son. If only Rashad would have taken the time to have listened, we wouldn't be standing in front of a judge today…

"You honor, I would like to work on our marriage and see if we can sort through our differences," I advised, while Rashad immediately shook his head. I couldn't believe how bad Rashad looked. He looked very weak and frail, as if he hasn't had a hot meal in years.

"No! Your Honor, we've done that. I'm asking that you grant my divorce, so I can get on with my life," Rashad responded as he began to cough.

I couldn't believe he was willing to throw me away like some piece of trash. Especially after all I'd done for him.

"Looking back on our records, it shows that Mr. King had filed for a divorce about five years-ago. Since then, you've constantly refused to sign the papers. With that being said, I have no other choice but to grant Mr. King a divorce. He's been patient this long and it's only right that I grant the divorce," he said as he hit his mallet.

"But Your Honor!" I cried as my voice trembled in disbelief. "I want my marriage!" I shrieked as the reality began to sink in. "Rashad, please!" I bawled as I watched him walk-out the courtroom, holding Stacey's hand.

"He's my husband!" I shouted at Stacey as my tears poured from my eyes. "I hate you!" I screamed as the Bailiff escorted me outside the courthouse.

I was devastated! I immediately drove to the home I once shared with Rashad. I waited by the front door for Rashad to get home. I was ready to spill all the tea. (*I should have said something sooner),* I regretted as I waited impatiently for Rashad.

*****

About two-hours later, Rashad and Stacey had pulled up.

"How could you!" I cried as I began to confront Rashad. "I'm pregnant!" I screamed as I pulled my shirt up to expose my pultruding belly.

"Congratulations, to you and whomever the father is," Rashad said as he bypassed me and opened the door.

"You are the father!" I fumed as I began hitting him in the back of his head.

"Get your hands off my husband!" Stacey shouted with rage.

"Excuse me?" I screamed as it felt like I swallowed down a huge sword that had cut my throat.

"Yes, my husband!" she emphasized as she exposed her diamond wedding band.

"What! But how?" I panted while I struggled to come into terms of what's been said.

"The courthouse," she proudly responded with a smirk on her face.

I knew right then Stacey was up to something, because she never dreamed of having a courthouse wedding. She was too bougie for that. Even when I suggested that Rashad and I get married at the courthouse, she cringed as if she was about to vomit.

"She's planning on killing you, Rashad!" I screamed as I pulled his hand so he'd listen.

Stacey looked like she'd been spooked.

"That's a lie!" she smirked as if I had gone crazy.

"Tia, can we please stop this? It's getting old. If you like it or not… I'm married to Rashad now. And I Junior's step mother. Now, if you don't mind, you're disturbing our honeymoon," she said as she quickly slammed the door in my face.

I felt so helpless, but the love I had for Rashad wouldn't allow me to give up just yet. No matter what a paper might say, Rashad will always and forever be, my man!

CHAPTER 19

It'd been almost two months, since I'd last seen my son and Rashad. I'm almost six-months pregnant. I'd been constantly sending letters to Rashad, but I still hadn't gotten a letter in return. I don't know if my son was okay and I hated myself for that. I promised my son that I would never leave him, but I failed miserably.

Today I'm getting dress for my ultrasound appointment. I'd been putting it off (*In hopes*) that Rashad would find it in his heart to come, but he hasn't. Just like today, I'll be finding out what we're having, alone. This made me realize how alone I really was in this big world. My only brother committed suicide when he'd learned our mother had finally passed from AIDS. My three half siblings don't even acknowledge me. It's sad, because my mother took them in and raised them as if they were her own kids. Those bastards weren't even present at my mother's funeral. Their mother was the reason for both of my parent's death. It was later confirmed that their mother was a prostitute and dad was one of her many clients. She was found beaten and burnt to death, shortly after dad had found out he tested positive. My poor mother, all she ever wanted to be was a great wife and mother, but dad's selfishness only caused her an early death sentence.

I pulled up to my appointment fifteen-minutes early. I walked to the building wearing my favorite flowered summer dress, although it was the beginning of November. The cool breeze felt wonderful as it blew between my legs. I quickly held my dress down so I didn't flash anyone as I walked inside. I finally made it in the building and signed in at the front desk. Shortly after, the ultrasound tech called my name. I smiled as I slowly I pulled myself on the table and laid back. I was so excited to know what I was having. I quickly pulled my summer dress over my baby bump. I couldn't believe how big I had grown.

I soon felt little kicks when the tech squeezed the warm gel on my belly.

"So, what are you hoping for?" She asks, as she rubbed the ultrasound-device across my stomach.

"I'm just praying for a healthy baby," I replied, but deep down I was wishing for a baby girl.

"Well… *SHE*, definitely appears to be healthy," she smiled, as she typed… "It's a Girl" on the ultrasound screen.

I almost jumped off the table in excitement! I couldn't believe Rashad and I were having our first girl! I couldn't help but to smile. *(Thank God)*, I smiled to myself.

Shortly after, a nurse walked in the room.

"Excuse me, I don't mean to interrupt, but the doctor needs to see you after you're finished," she said with a strange look on her face.

"Is everything okay?" I quickly asked as my smile was now replaced with fear.

"Yes, the doctor just need to speak with you," she said as she quickly exited the room.

After confirming the baby was growing fine, the tech helped me up and handed me a few ultrasound pictures of my daughter. I couldn't help but to smile proudly as I stared at her adorable little hands and feet.

Before I left, I quickly walked to the front and waited for my doctor as, requested. Shortly after, the nurse called me to go back. I waited in the small cold room for what seemed like twenty minutes, before the doctor finally walked in. She had a very weird look on her face, causing my worry.

"Is something wrong with my baby?" I immediately asked.

"Mrs. King, the reason why I requested to speak to you is because of the recent lab work you had done."

"Please don't tell me I have chlamydia?" I begged as I thought about how foolish I was not to have used a condom with Rashad.

"Well, actually your lab test came back negative for chlamydia," she quickly explained.

"Thank God!" I shouted with relief to have dodged a bullet, because this wouldn't have been the first-time Rashad had given me an STD.

"Wait, Tia… there's more," she revealed, causing my heart to sink to my chest.

"Well, what is it?" I quickly asked as I held my breath.

"Tia, you've tested positive for HIV."

That was all I remembered before I collapsed. I woke up in a hospital bed with an IV inside my arm. Shortly after, my doctor walked in.

"How are you feeling, Tia?' The Doctor gently-asked as she stood over me.

"How I feel? You told me I have HIV!" I screamed horrified as the words alone haunted me.

"I'm sorry Tia, but I had to make you aware. You are pregnant and it's very important that you start treatment immediately," she said firmly.

The whole room began to spin as I closed my eyes.

"This has to be a joke! Please tell me you're joking? Please!" I begged.

"I'm sorry Tia, I wish it wasn't true, but unfortunately it is. You are HIV positive," she said very firmly, causing me to scream out in horror.

"Tia, Calm down. Everything's going to be okay," she said in a very calming tone as she gently-touched my hand.

"Okay? How is everything going to be okay when you told me I have HIV?" I shouted in anger.

"With the proper treatment and medicine, you can live a long and healthy life," she assured me.

"But chances are my daughter can still be born with the disease, right?" I said as I tried to come to terms with the reality of my baby being born with a deadly disease.

"Unfortunately, I can't say there's a hundred percent chance that she won't be born with it. But, I will say… with proper treatment and taking your medicine routinely will give her a good fighting chance," she explained, but deep inside the truth still remained… I have HIV and there's a chance of my baby girl contracting the disease as well. There's just no way I could take the risk of my daughter being born with HIV because of the bad choices I've made.

"Thank you, and if that is all… I like to leave now," I quickly responded as I waited for my doctor to reply.

"Yes, Tia… You're free to go. But remember, I need you back tomorrow morning so we can start your treatment. We're going to do our best to assure your daughter isn't born with it. But to do that, we need your full participation in this. I know you're upset, but please… Think about you daughter, please!" she begged as she pulled the I.V from out my arm and covered it with a Band-Aid.

"Tia, are you listening?" The Doctor asked, as she looked at me very strangely.

"Yes, I hear you! If you don't mind, I'd like to leave now?" I said as I became very impatient.

"Yes Tia, you can go. But please remember, I need to see you first thing tomorrow morning," she warned as I walked out the door.

I was so devastated, I walked straight past the front desk.

"Excuse me, Mrs. King. You forgot to schedule your next appointment," the receptionist shouted.

"My next appointment won't be necessary," I assured her as I headed for the elevator.

Once I made it to my car, I broke down and started crying. I thought about how stupid I was to have contracted HIV. My mother and I were more alike than one. We both loved our husbands so much, we contracted a death-sentence to prove our love. The only difference was, she died from the AIDS virus. It was pitiful that we could love our husbands that damn much! I couldn't believe I let my love for Rashad impair my judgement. I already knew that Stacey was a big-time hoe. I should have run and never looked back the minute I found out they were messing around, but no, I just had to have him regardless of anything. Now I'm left pregnant with a deadly disease from the very same man, I still love. Unfortunately, I still loved Rashad, and if we both have this disease, we should at least die together. I battled with my thoughts as I thought about the words of our pastor on our wedding day.

"To death do us part," I whispered as I wiped my tears from my eyes. (*I must make Rashad aware of his health and show him that Stacey ain't shit. Only then, will he divorce her ass and realize the mistake he made, and how much he really needs me*), I thought long and hard to myself, as I finally drove-off to make things right.

CHAPTER 20

I unlocked the door to my motel room. It was a little after six o'clock when I slowly walked in. I had been driving for hours debating whether I should do it. After a long debate, I'd come to the decision to do it. I wiped my tears as I popped a Vicodin, I'd bought from the old lady a couple doors down. She was always selling her pain meds for a fix. I never condoned her doing that, but today, I had no other choice but to buy her whole strip. I knew I would be in terrible pain. I slowly wiped my tears as I pulled a metal hanger off a pair of my skinny jeans. I waited about thirty-minutes for the Vicodin to take full effect, before I ran a hot bath to soak in. I needed to be comfortable. I also took the small Bible laying on the motel's end table inside the bathroom with me. I slowly got on my knees and turned the Bible to John 1:9

"If we confess our sins, he is faithful and just to forgive us [our] sins, and to cleanse us from all unrighteousness."

I recited as I began to feel very sleepy as the medicine started to kick in. I slowly got off my knees and submerged my body into the warm bath as if I was getting baptized of all my sins. I had witnessed Big-Mary do this many times in prison. My cellmate Rebecca had made Big-Mary prison rich as many times she had her to perform a Jailhouse abortion on her. Or else, almost every male guard in prison would have a child from her. Although, I never saw anyone try to attempt one on their self, I knew it couldn't be that hard. I slowly picked the hanger out of the bathroom sink, I had soaking in hot water I'd mixed with two bottles of alcohol. I slowly rubbed the metal hanger and my vagina with K-Y Jelly to lubricate it. I closed my eyes and prayed to God as I spread my legs over the sides of the tub. As I continued to pray, I slowly lowered the hanger to my vagina and raised my hips. I then took a deep breath as I slowly began to insert the hanger inside of my vagina. I was interrupted by two hard kicks to my belly which startled me as I quickly opened my eyes.

"I can't do it!" I screamed as I slung the hanger across the bathroom floor.

"I'm sorry baby, I'm so sorry!" I cried as I gently rubbed my pregnant belly. My daughter was a gift from God and I had no choice but to live with whatever the outcome was.

I quickly got out the tub and dried off.

"I have to see Rashad tonight!" I said to myself as I quickly got dressed and grabbed my purse as I walked-out my motel room.

CHAPTER 21

I arrived to Rashad's house a little after ten o'clock. I had a look of horror on my face as I noticed the 2010 Range Rover parked in the driveway. I knew right then something wasn't right. I quickly cut off the ignition and slowly opened and closed my car door. I stood at the front door to see if I could hear voices inside. I heard the same man's voice that Stacey would always meet inside the house. He didn't sound like a house-guest. He seemed very pissed. I knew right then that Rashad and my son needed my help. I slowly snuck myself to the back of our home. I knew Junior always left the side-door unlocked and I prayed he did tonight. Just like I prayed for, the side door was unlocked.

My heart blasted heavy-beats through my chest, as I slowly put my trembling hands on the doorknob. After taking a deep breath, I finally opened the side door. I immediately pissed my pants when the door began to squeak. I quickly tiptoed to the laundry room when I heard the man yell for Stacey to go and check it out. Without hesitation, Stacey made her way downstairs in her Chanel pumps. I listened to every clicking-step she made as she finally made it to the side door and looked around to see if anyone was outside. I watched from the dark laundry-room as she quickly locked the door.

"I'm going to fuck his little ass up, too!" She snarled as she marched back upstairs.

I felt my heart leave my chest when I heard her threatened to hurt my son. I quickly dialed 911 and told them to come quick as I hung-up the phone and cut it off. I didn't want them to call my phone back while I was sneaking up on Stacey and them. I said a quick prayer to God as I slowly made my way up the stairs. My legs were shaking so badly as I carefully climbed each stair. I could hear the man shouting at Rashad.

"You murdered my sister, mother fucker!" he shouted as I heard a loud sound right after. (*Omg, that's Nina's brother*), I said to myself. Nina was the side-chick Rashad had beaten before he killed her by shooting her three-times in the back of her head, which I took the charge for. I couldn't believe it, as I held my hand over my mouth not to scream.

"Don't kill my daddy!" I heard Junior begin to scream. I had to catch myself as I felt my feet about to give way. I couldn't believe they would involve my son in this madness.

"Shut the fuck up lil nigga, before I murder your ass first!'" he warned as Rashad immediately began to beg for our son's life. By this time, I had made it to the doorway. I watched as my son and Rashad laid on the bedroom floor tied-up, while Stacey laid across the bed with a smile on her face.

"Nigga, he going to die just like Nina and that's going to be the last thing you watch before you die."

"Man, I'll give you fifty-stacks if you just let my son go," Rashad pleaded with him, but that didn't seem to motivate him at all!

"Man, I don't give a damn about fifty stacks!" he shouted as he hocked up spit from the back of his throat and spitted it directly in Rashad's face. He then put duct-tape over Rashad and my son's mouths while Stacey smiled with enjoyment.

"Please don't kill my son!" I screamed before I knew it. I stood frozen looking like a deer in headlights as the man now pointed his gun at me.

"Who the hell is this bitch?" he immediately asked Stacey as she got out of bed and stood next to him.

"That's Rashad's ex-wife, and oh, she's also my ex-best friend," she smirked as she looked over at me.

"Please, just let them go. The police are on the way," I pleaded as I stuttered through every one of my words.

"Does it look like I give a damn about the fuckin' police? I came prepared to die!" he confessed, causing chills to crawled up my spine.

"Please, you don't have to do this," I begged as I got down on my knees.

"Kill that bitch first," Stacey encouraged as she tried to convince Nina's brother to kill me.

"Hell nawl, I'm not killing no pregnant woman. If you want her dead, you must do that shit your damn self. I'm only going to hell with two bodies. That's this nigga and his punk ass son," he explained, causing me to feel very weak as if I would pass out at any time. I knew right then, I had to confess.

"It was me, I killed your sister!' I revealed as my nerves was raging with fear.

I watched as Nina's brother's eyes lit up in shock.

"Hell nawl, it wasn't you. You just did time for his punk-ass. What kind of nigga let his own damn wife do time for his bitch ass? Only A punk ass nigga would!" he shouted as he kicked Rashad in his stomach, causing his shake in pain.

Just then, flickers of lights shined through our bedroom window. I knew it was the police as we heard loud knocks on the front and back door.

"Oh shit! That bitch really did call the fuckin police," Stacey began to panic as she ran around the bedroom, grabbing up her things.

"Put those fuckin' bags down!" the man's voice thundered like lightening, causing Stacey to stop dead in her tracks. "You not going anywhere!" he warned as Stacey's eyes looked like she'd seen Satan himself.

"Quit playing, Dee! I did my part," she said as she began to pick her bags from off the bedroom floor.

"Bitch, I'm dying with no witnesses!' he said very calmly this time, as he slowly pointed his gun to Stacey's head.

"Dee, are you crazy!" she screamed in fear as her bony legs began to shake.

Dee just stared at her for a few seconds before he finally responded.

"I refuse to let you walk out this door alive. You are truly the devil in disguise. You are as venomous as a snake," he said as he continued to stare at her.

"What the hell are you talking about, Dee?" she shouted as she stared at him in fear.

"The gift you possess is deadly. My only question to you baby, is how do you carry it so damn well?"

"Carry what?" she shouted, as she waited on Dee to respond.

After a few seconds, Dee responded…

"AIDS, bitch!" he coldly revealed. The look in Rashad's eyes was something I'd never seen before. I couldn't place an emotion on it. I also watched as Stacey looked as if she was busted. After a few seconds of silence, Stacey took a deep breath as she ran her fingers through her long Brazilian weave.

"So, that's what this is about?" she asked very calm and boldly as she looked at Dee without a grain of pity.

"Bitch! What the fuck you mean, is that's what this is about? You gave me AIDS, bitch!" he said as his anger intensified.

Just then, there was a huge bang at the front and back door as the police tried to kick open the doors.

"So!" Stacey shouted as she smacked her lips. "Someone gave the shit to me. I didn't ask for this shit, but do you see me crying like a little bitch?" she said as she was now wearing a smile on her face.

After a brief silence, Dee miraculously lowered his gun and took a deep breath as Stacey continued to smile.

"No, I don't see you crying like a little bitch," Dee said very calmly as he stared into her fake blue eyes.

Just then, Dee slowly pointed the gun back at Stacey's head. Her smile had now disappeared and was replaced with a new look of horror.

"But you're going to eat this bullet like the little bitch you are!" he finally spoke as he shot Stacey twice in her face. I watched as Stacey's brains splattered everywhere! The same place Nina's brains had splattered ten years-ago. Just then there was a loud bang as the front door was finally kicked in. I heard the footsteps of police officers making their way inside our home.

"We're upstairs!" I shouted the minute I heard them swarming the house.

Dee just stood in silence looking up at the ceiling before he finally responded.

"Nina, this is for you baby!" He shouted as he slowly pointed his gun over to Rashad and my son.

Before the gunshot went off, I ran as fast as I could to cover them.

Bang, bang, bang! That was the last thing I heard as I laid over my son and Rashad, bleeding to death. I could also see Dee laying on the floor dead while blood poured from his body.

I watched as the officers, removed my son from the crime scene. I watched as Rashad fought his way next to me and held my dying hand.

"Baby, I'm so sorry," he wept, as he held his stomach from the pain he felt.

"Please Tia, don't die!" he cried out as he put pressure on the wounds to my upper chest.

"Someone call the ambulance, please!" he begged as he tightly held my hand, but it was too late. I felt my body getting cold and breathing became hard to do. The only thing left to do, was to say… "I love you," as I closed my eyes and died right in Rashad's arms.

CHAPTER 22

I watched my funeral from heaven. I watched how Rashad cried over my coffin and wished for God to take him instead. I watched how the pastor prayed for him, how our son cried, and how Rashad wished he had died.

"I can't believe I'm dead!"

As I hear you screaming my name in the middle of the night. Like I would appear and hold you tight. I watched how you passionately sniffed the scent from my lingerie, and how you begged me to come back to you. I even heard you apologize a million-times for the million-times you made me cry from all your lies. I also saw all the flowers you put on my grave, even though it wasn't my birthday or a holiday. If only you could have sent those flowers those other days, I would have loved them even more. You even prayed to God every night for me to forgive you, but what you don't know is, I have. I just wished you have told me and showed me sooner, when I was alive, so I could feel the love and joy of you by my side.

I whispered as you dreamed, or maybe it's a nightmare? As I watch you twist and turn and yell out my name, the name that once brought you nothing but pain, but I still tell you to sleep tight, because I'll still watch over you at night. I watched as you pulled your covers tight as if the guilt continues to haunt you at night, but don't worry my love. I still love you and always will!" I had whispered in your ear before I finally disappeared. I watched you jump out your sleep, searching for me! Then you broke down to your knees as tears ran from your cheeks.

"Tia, Tia, Tia!" you cried out for me.

But me coming to you will never ever be. Now wipe your tears and just let it be…because you and I both know, you never deserved me. So just let me go, but you and I both know, there will never be another me… I'll always be your biggest fan and…

I'll always be down for my man.

CPSIA information can be obtained
at www.ICGtesting.com
Printed in the USA
LVOW10s2027270417
532438LV00014B/380/P